BABYMOUSE AND FRIENDS*

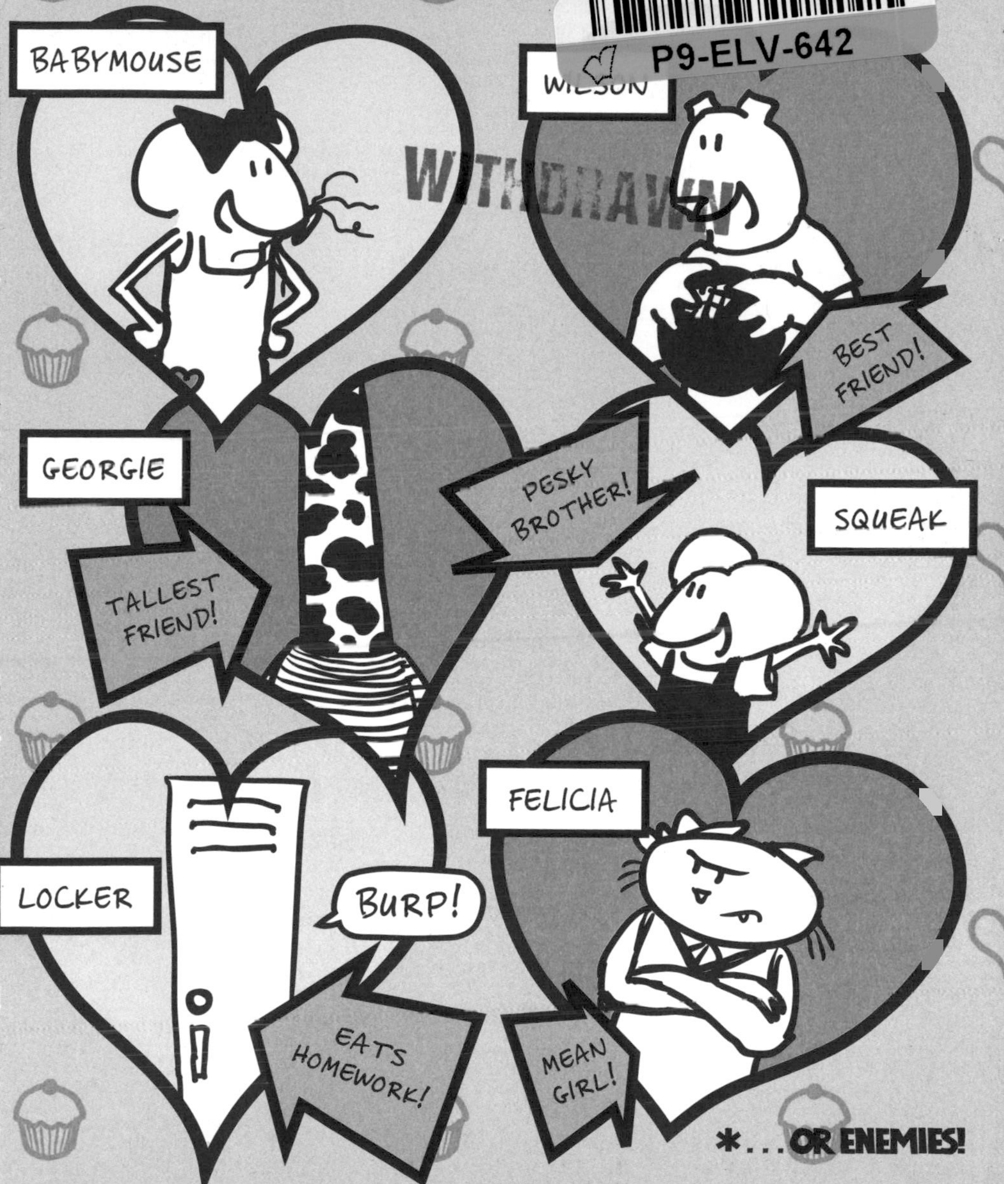
BABYMOUSE
WILSON
BEST FRIEND!
GEORGIE
TALLEST FRIEND!
PESKY BROTHER!
SQUEAK
LOCKER
BURP!
EATS HOMEWORK!
FELICIA
MEAN GIRL!

*...OR ENEMIES!

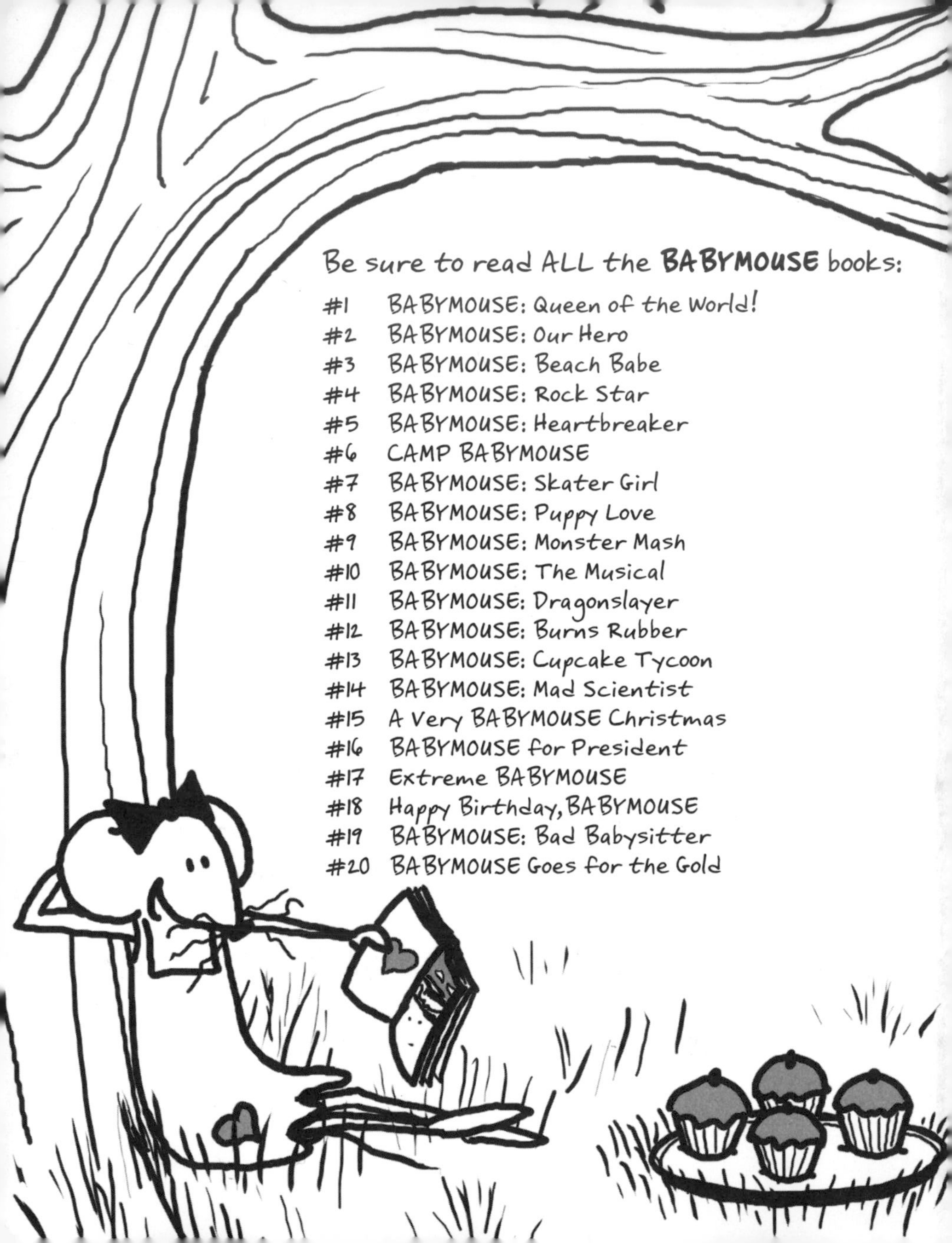

Be sure to read ALL the **BABYMOUSE** books:

- #1 BABYMOUSE: Queen of the World!
- #2 BABYMOUSE: Our Hero
- #3 BABYMOUSE: Beach Babe
- #4 BABYMOUSE: Rock Star
- #5 BABYMOUSE: Heartbreaker
- #6 CAMP BABYMOUSE
- #7 BABYMOUSE: Skater Girl
- #8 BABYMOUSE: Puppy Love
- #9 BABYMOUSE: Monster Mash
- #10 BABYMOUSE: The Musical
- #11 BABYMOUSE: Dragonslayer
- #12 BABYMOUSE: Burns Rubber
- #13 BABYMOUSE: Cupcake Tycoon
- #14 BABYMOUSE: Mad Scientist
- #15 A Very BABYMOUSE Christmas
- #16 BABYMOUSE for President
- #17 Extreme BABYMOUSE
- #18 Happy Birthday, BABYMOUSE
- #19 BABYMOUSE: Bad Babysitter
- #20 BABYMOUSE Goes for the Gold

BABYMOUSE
BEACH BABE

BY JENNIFER L. HOLM & MATTHEW HOLM

RANDOM HOUSE 🏠 NEW YORK

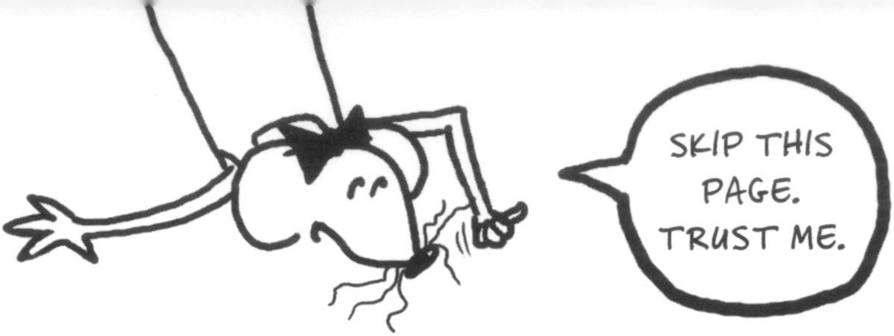
SKIP THIS PAGE. TRUST ME.

This is a work of fiction. Names, characters, places, and incidents either are the product of the authors' imagination or are used fictitiously. Any resemblance to actual persons, living or dead, events, or locales is entirely coincidental.

Published in the United States by Random House Children's Books, a division of Penguin Random House LLC, New York.

Random House and the colophon are registered trademarks of Penguin Random House LLC.

Visit us on the Web!
randomhousekids.com
Babymouse.com

Educators and librarians, for a variety of teaching tools, visit us at
RHTeachersLibrarians.com

Library of Congress Cataloging-in-Publication Data
Holm, Jennifer L.
Babymouse : beach babe / Jennifer L. Holm and Matthew Holm.
p. cm.
ISBN 978-0-375-83231-4 (trade) — ISBN 978-0-375-93231-1 (lib. bdg.) —
ISBN 978-0-307-97928-5 (ebook)
1. Graphic novels. I. Holm, Matthew. II. Title.
PN6727.H592B25 2006 741.5'973—dc22 2005046465

MANUFACTURED IN MALAYSIA 20 19 18 17 16 15

Random House Children's Books supports the First Amendment and celebrates the right to read.

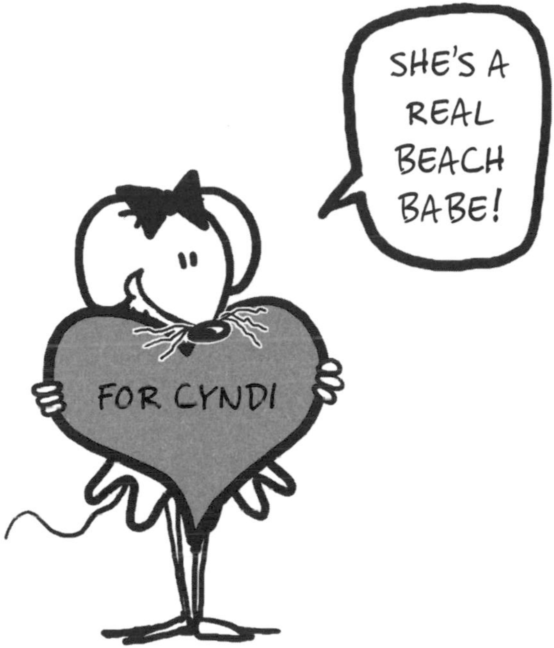
SHE'S A REAL BEACH BABE!
FOR CYNDI

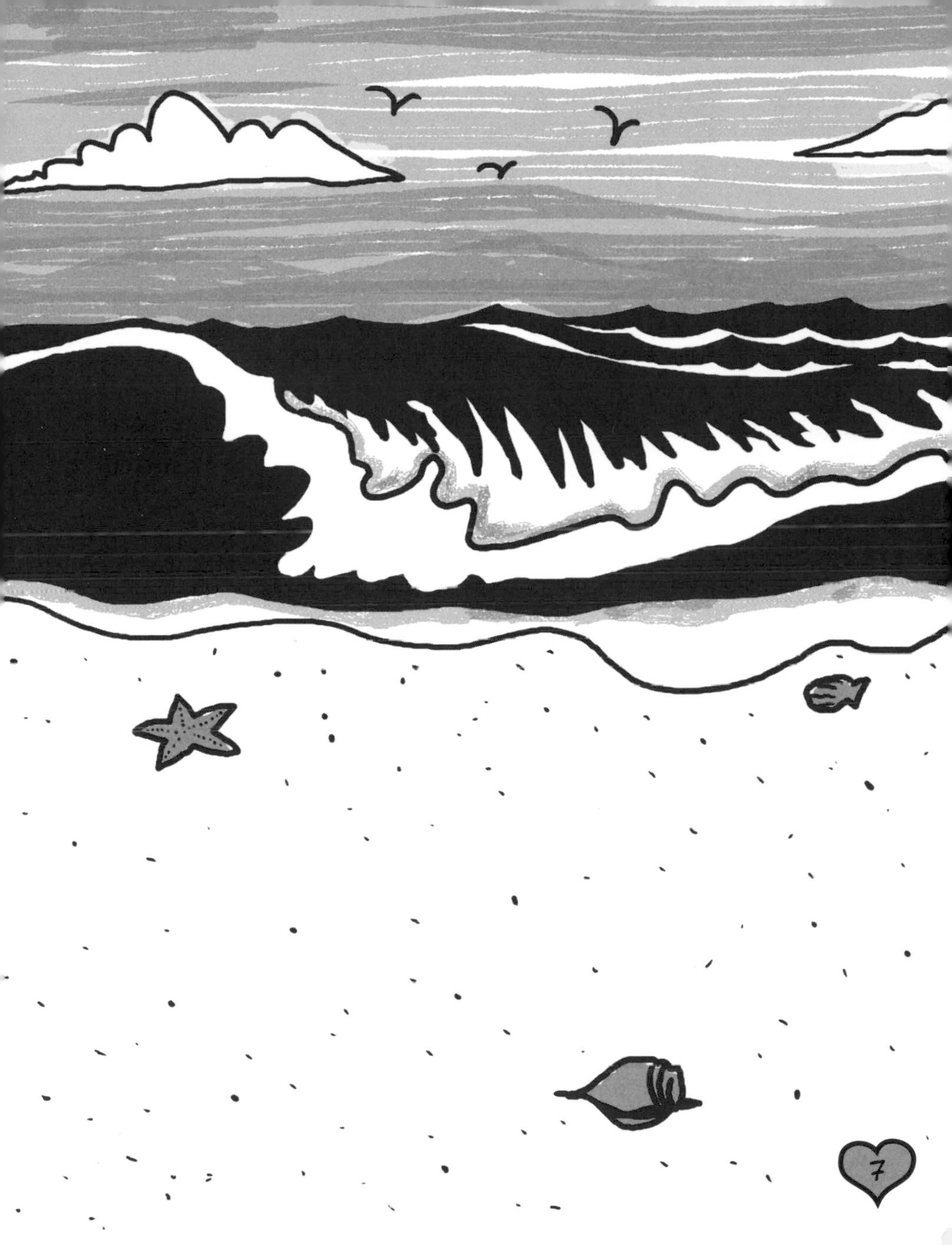

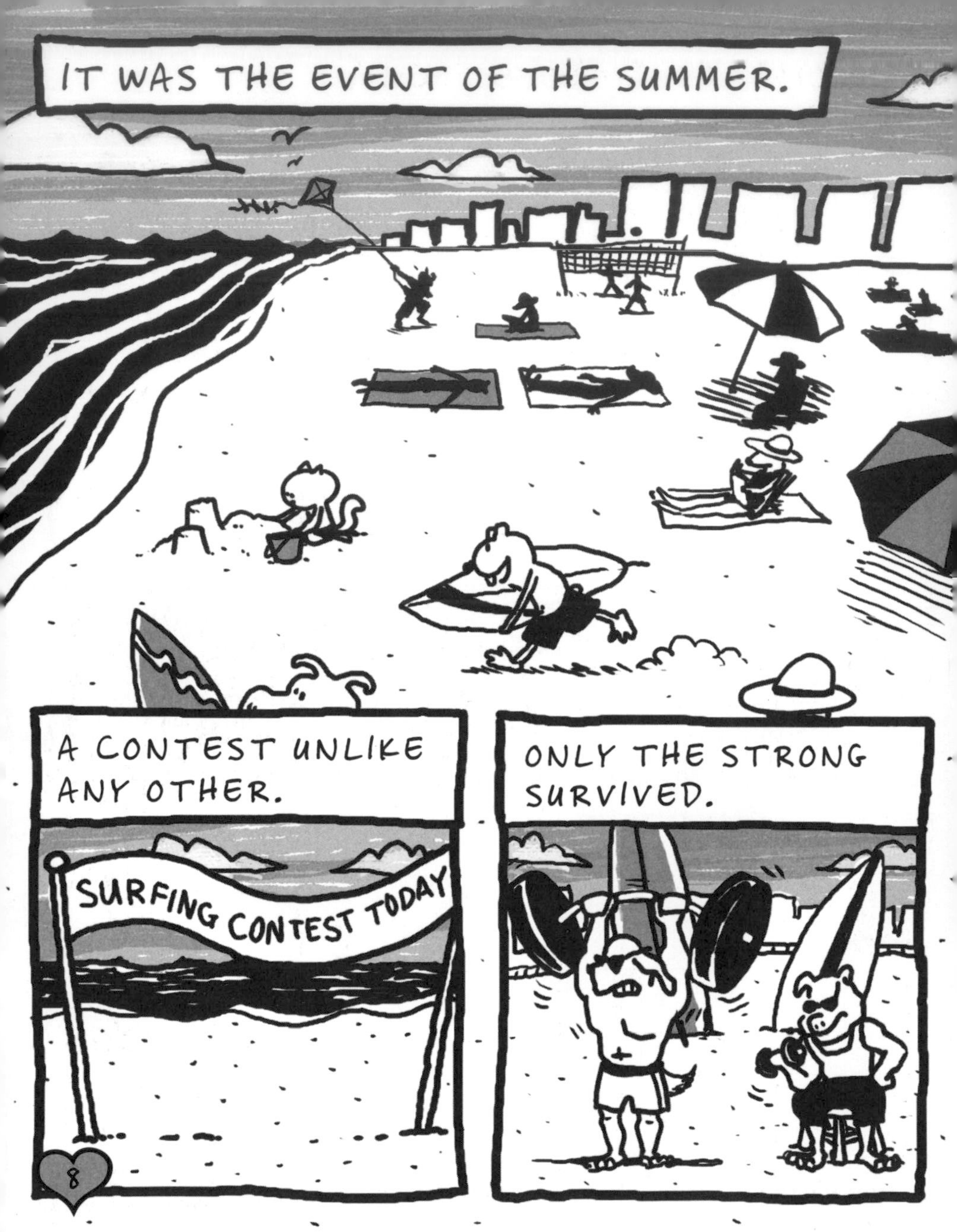
IT WAS THE EVENT OF THE SUMMER.
A CONTEST UNLIKE ANY OTHER.
SURFING CONTEST TODAY
ONLY THE STRONG SURVIVED.

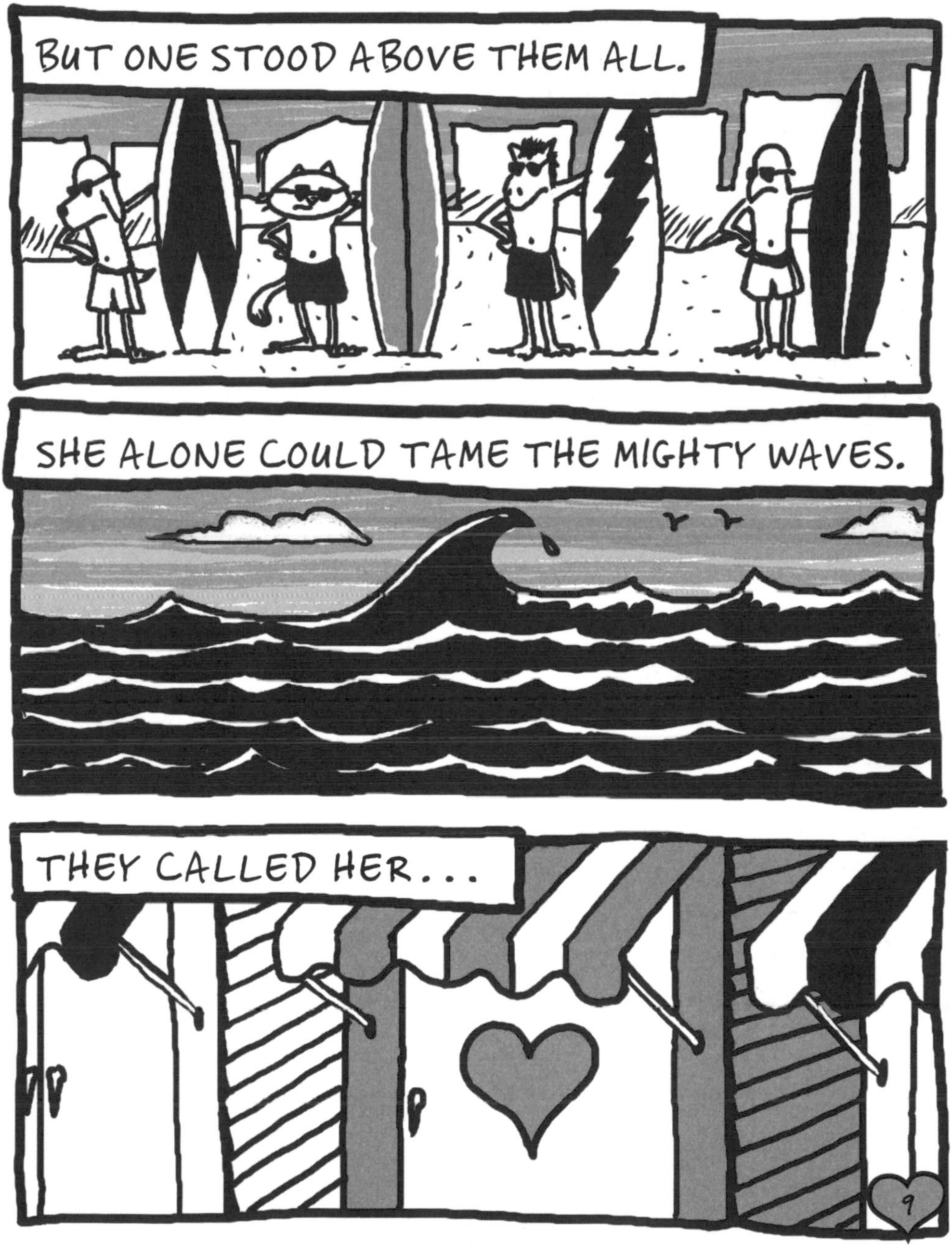
BUT ONE STOOD ABOVE THEM ALL.
SHE ALONE COULD TAME THE MIGHTY WAVES.
THEY CALLED HER...
9

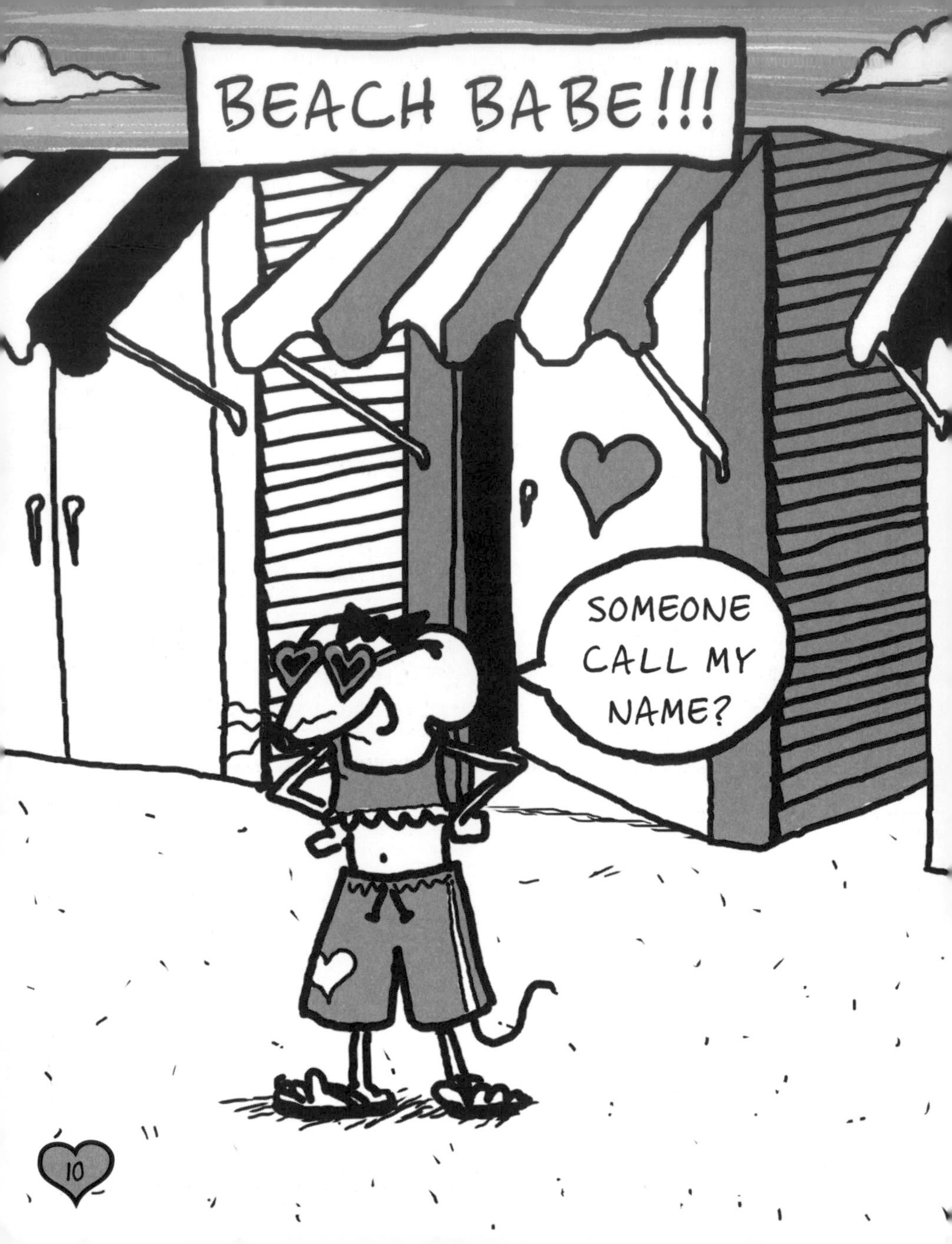
BEACH BABE!!!
SOMEONE CALL MY NAME?

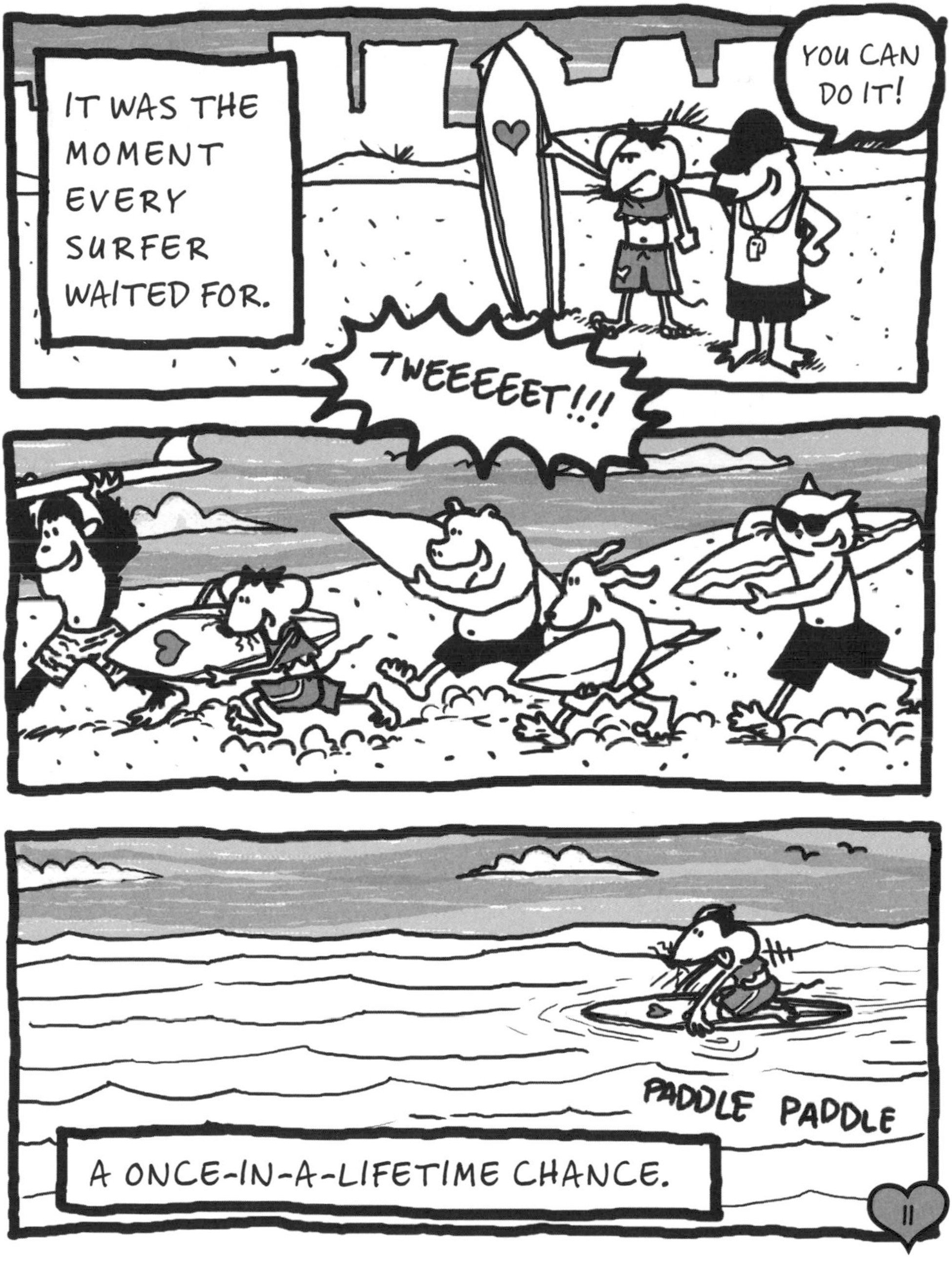
IT WAS THE MOMENT EVERY SURFER WAITED FOR.
YOU CAN DO IT!
TWEEEEEET!!!
PADDLE PADDLE
A ONCE-IN-A-LIFETIME CHANCE.

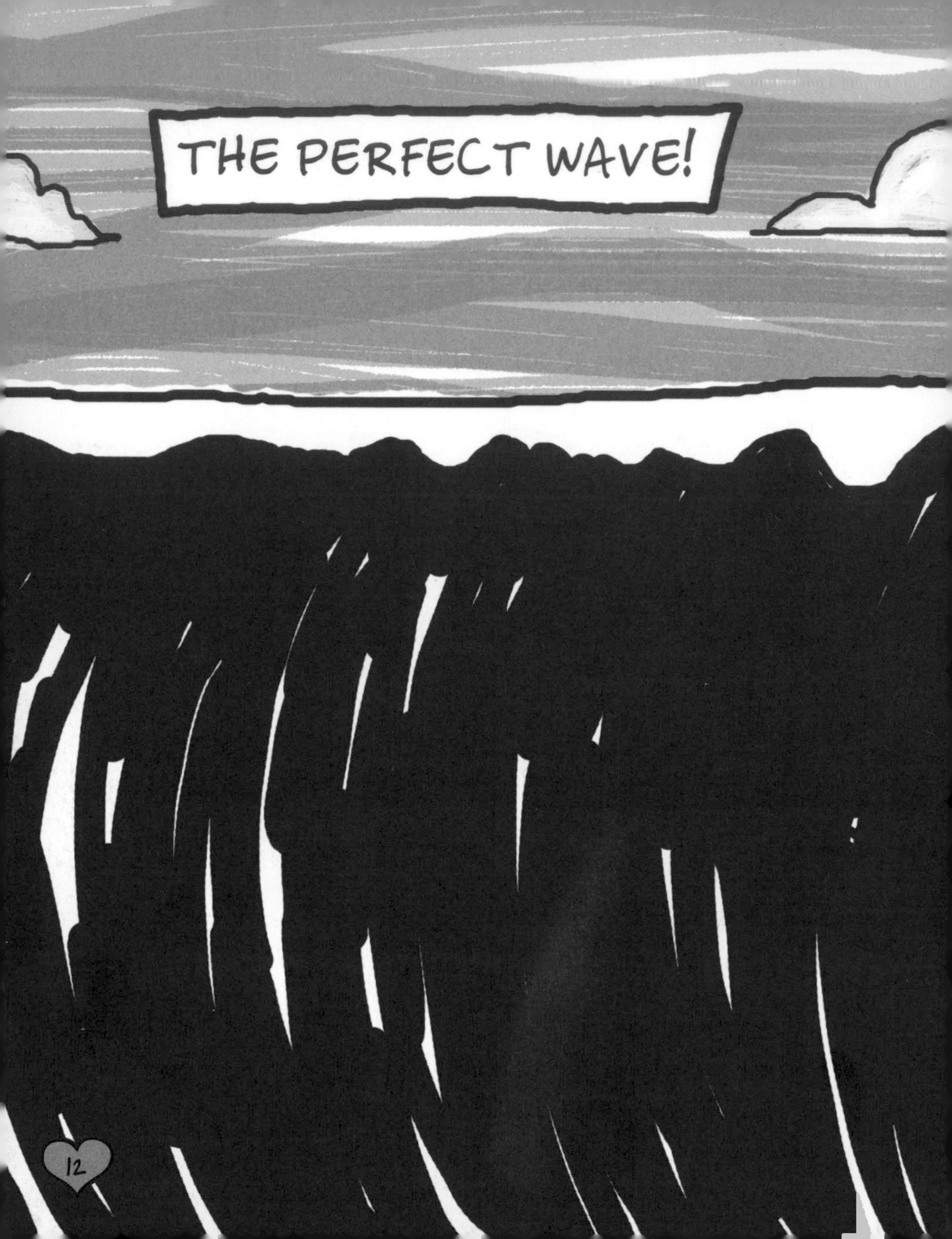
THE PERFECT WAVE!

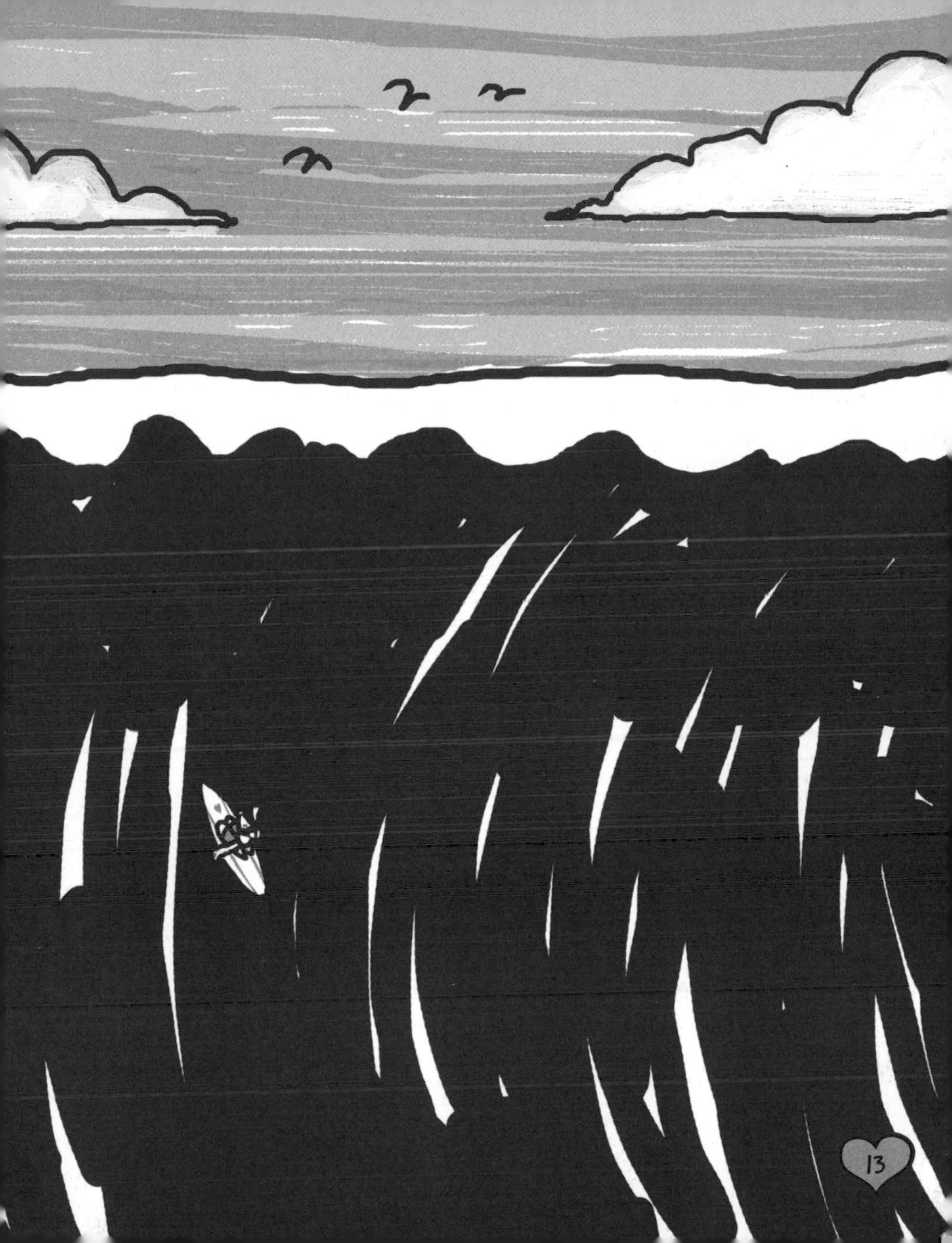

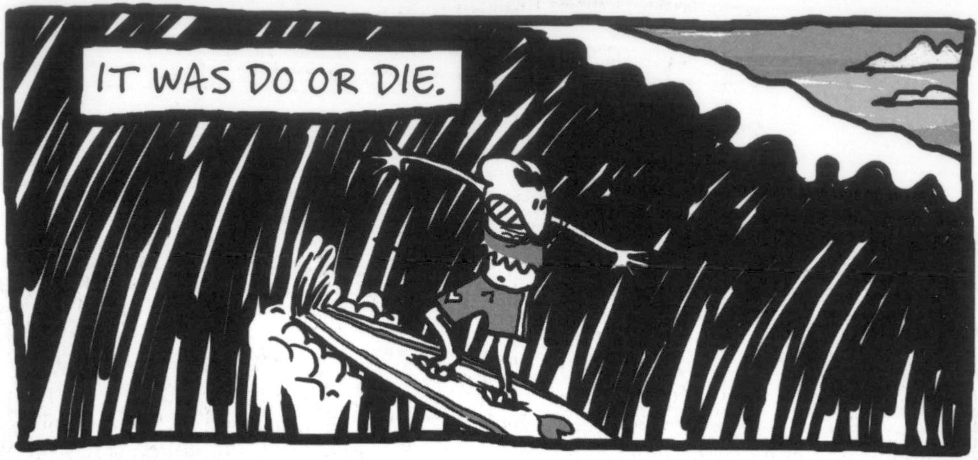
IT WAS DO OR DIE.

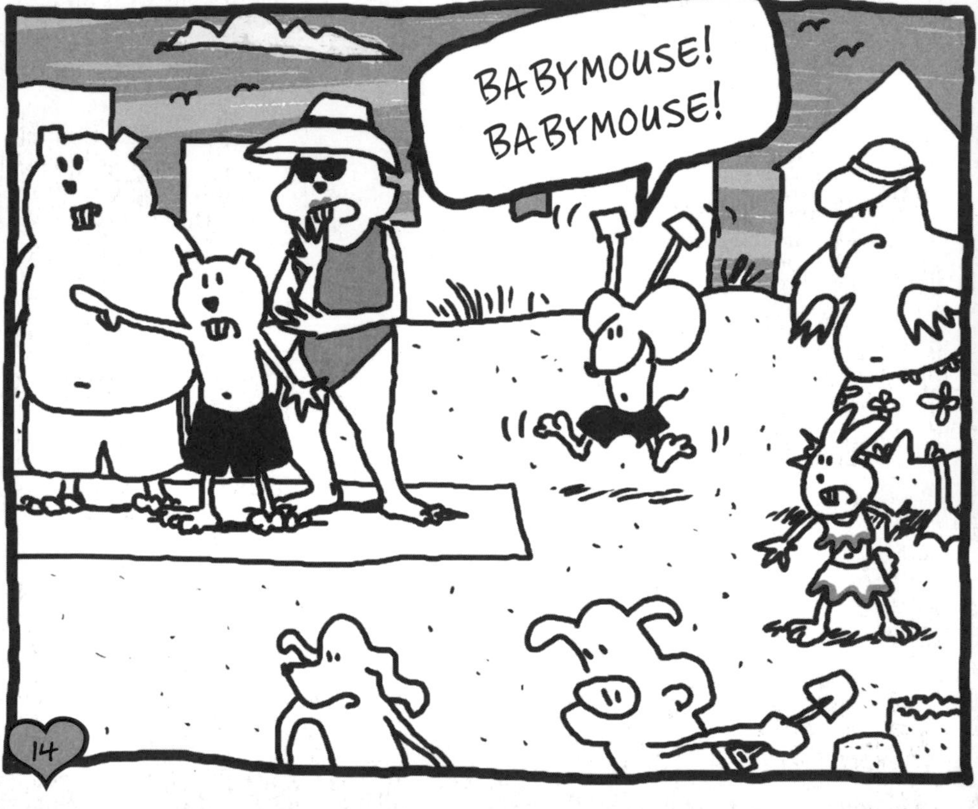
BABYMOUSE!
BABYMOUSE!

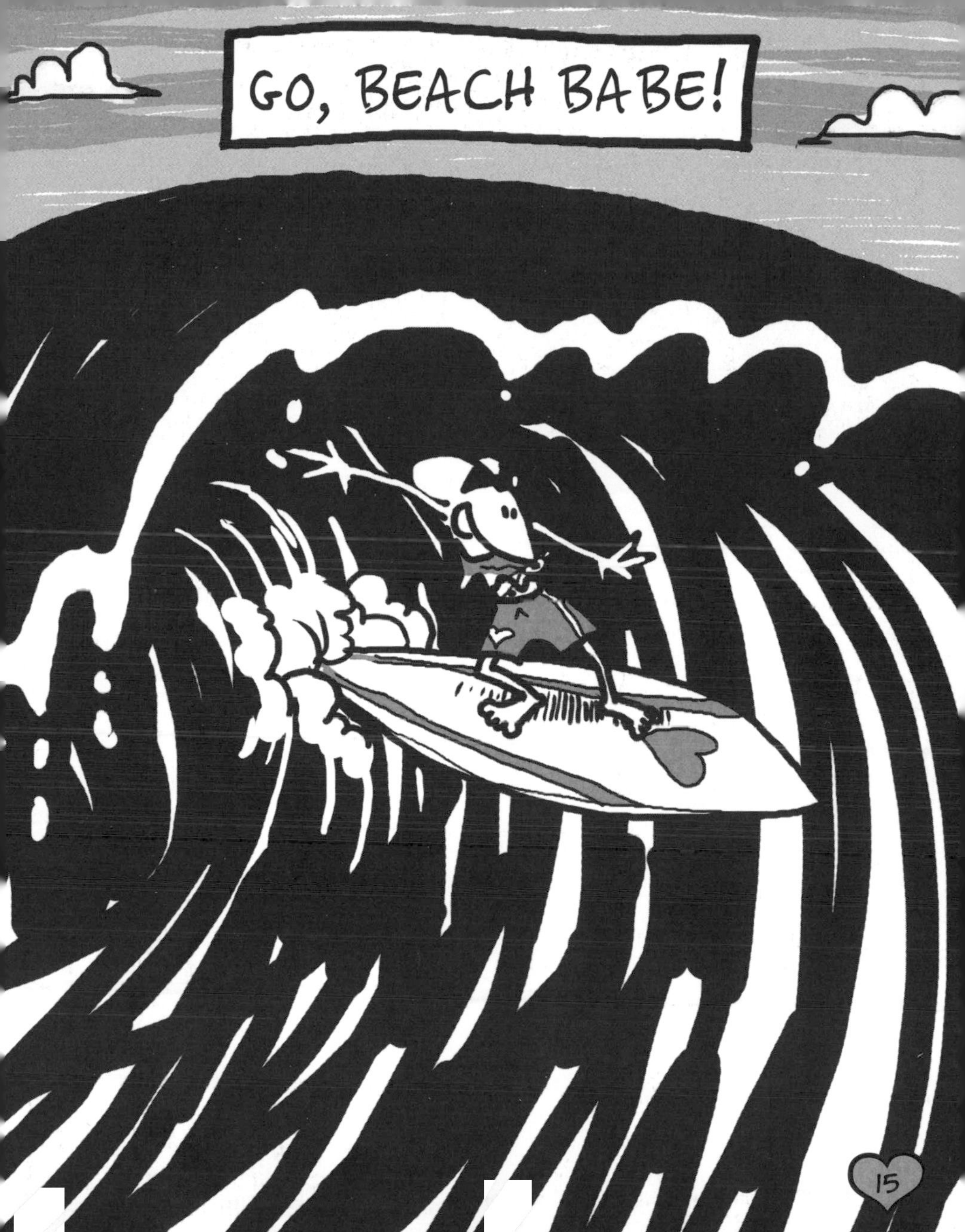
GO, BEACH BABE!

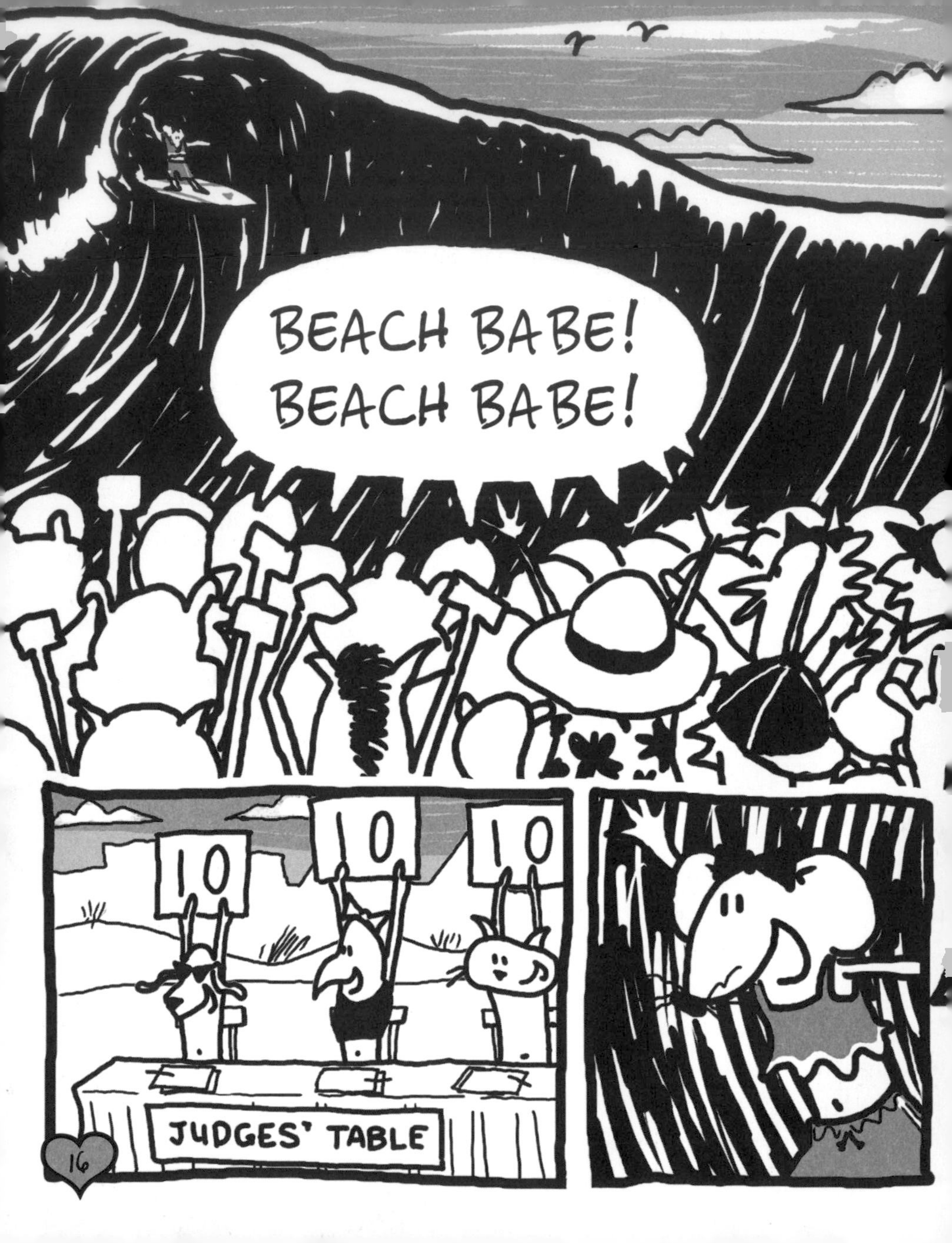
BEACH BABE! BEACH BABE!
10
10
10
JUDGES' TABLE

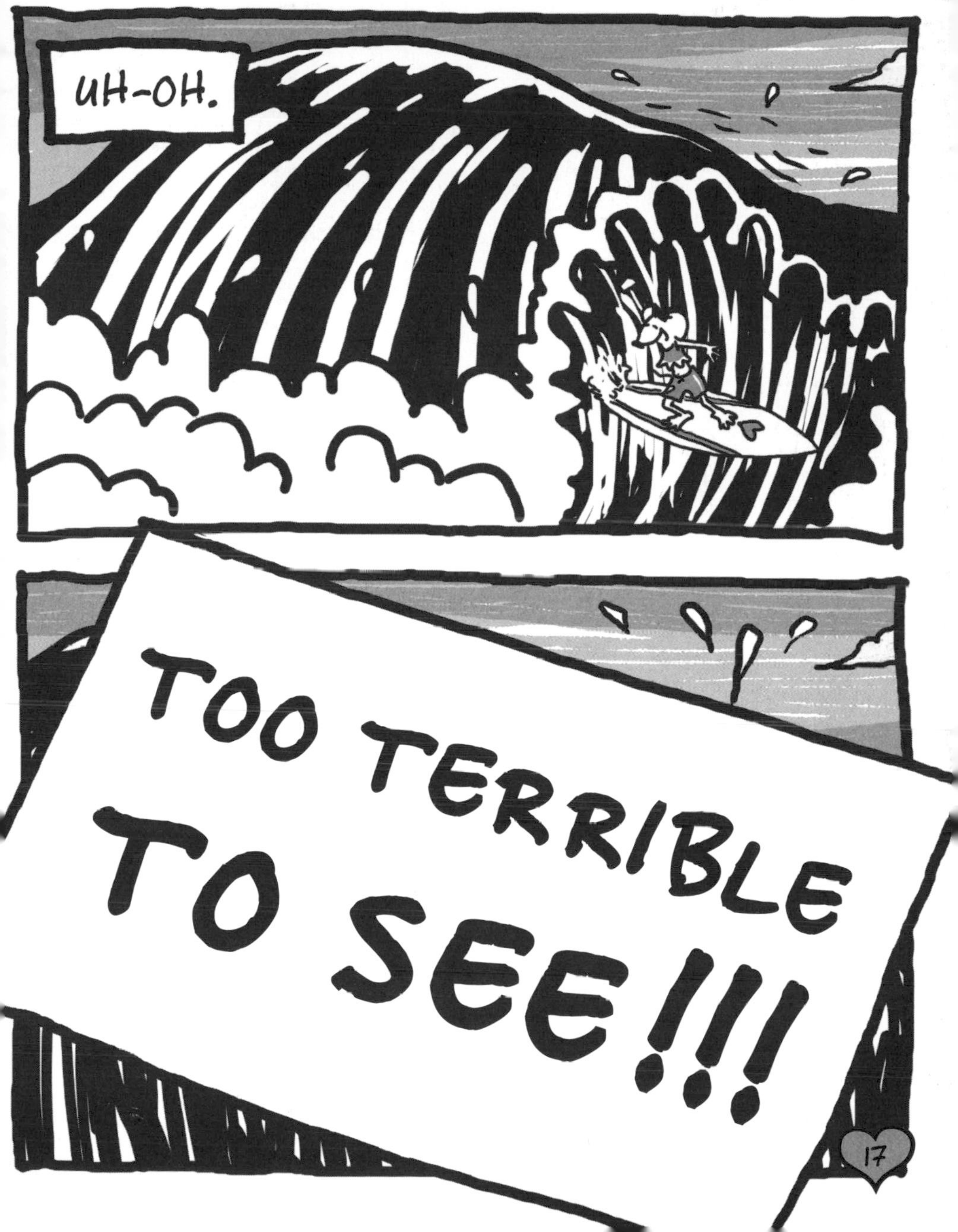
UH-OH.
TOO TERRIBLE TO SEE!!!

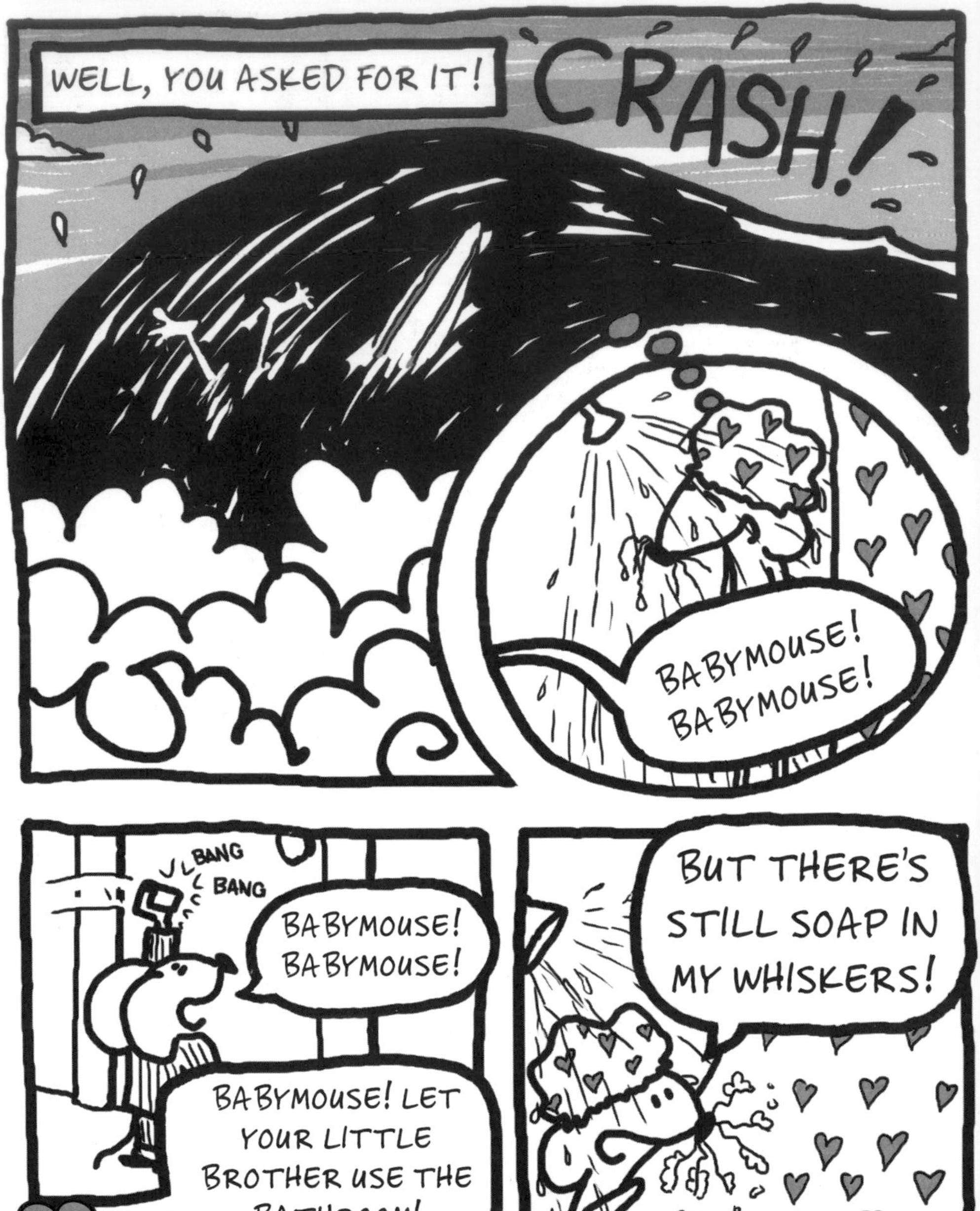
WELL, YOU ASKED FOR IT!
CRASH!
BABYMOUSE! BABYMOUSE!
BANG
BANG
BABYMOUSE! BABYMOUSE!
BABYMOUSE! LET YOUR LITTLE BROTHER USE THE BATHROOM!
BUT THERE'S STILL SOAP IN MY WHISKERS!

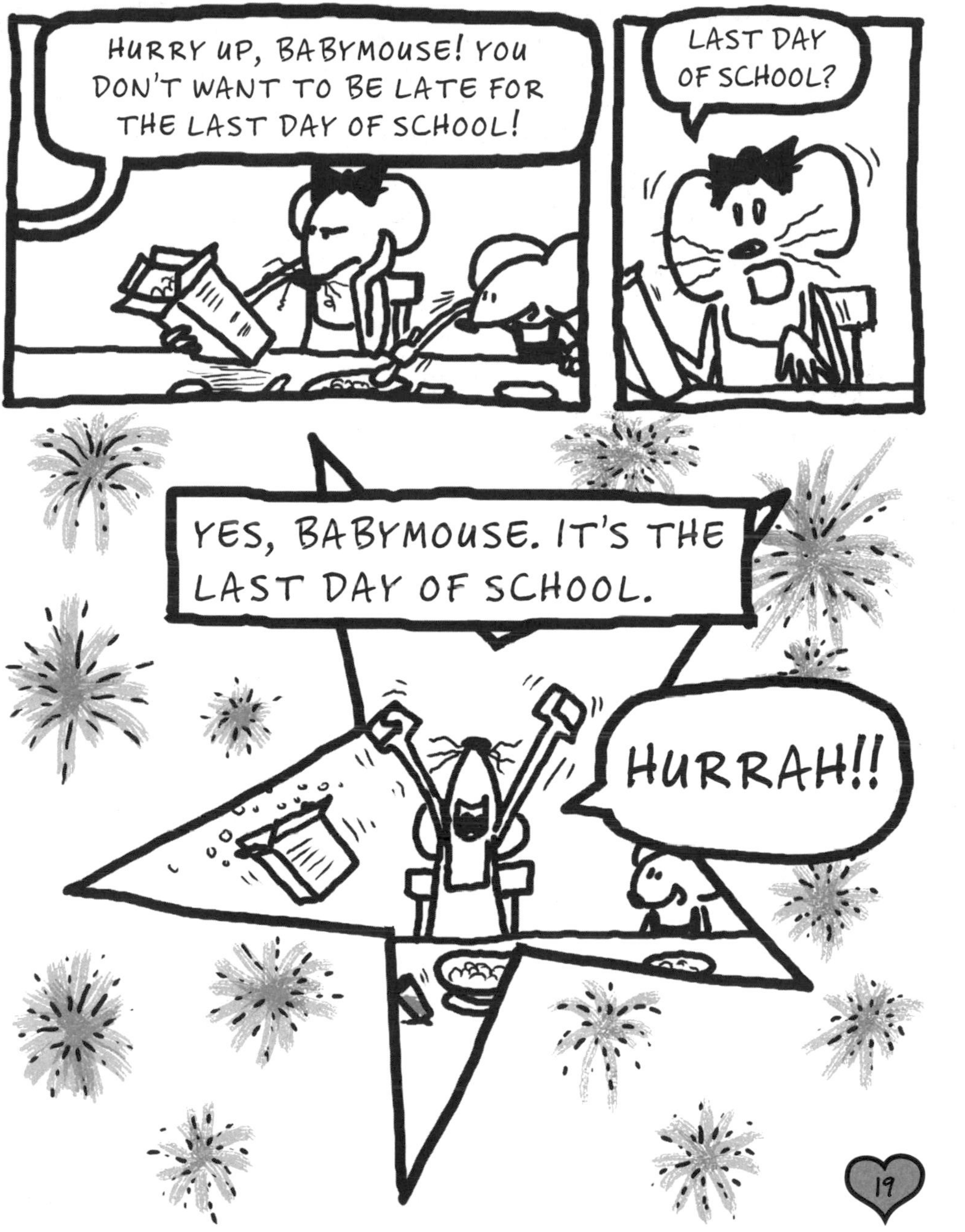
HURRY UP, BABYMOUSE! YOU DON'T WANT TO BE LATE FOR THE LAST DAY OF SCHOOL!
LAST DAY OF SCHOOL?
YES, BABYMOUSE. IT'S THE LAST DAY OF SCHOOL.
HURRAH!!

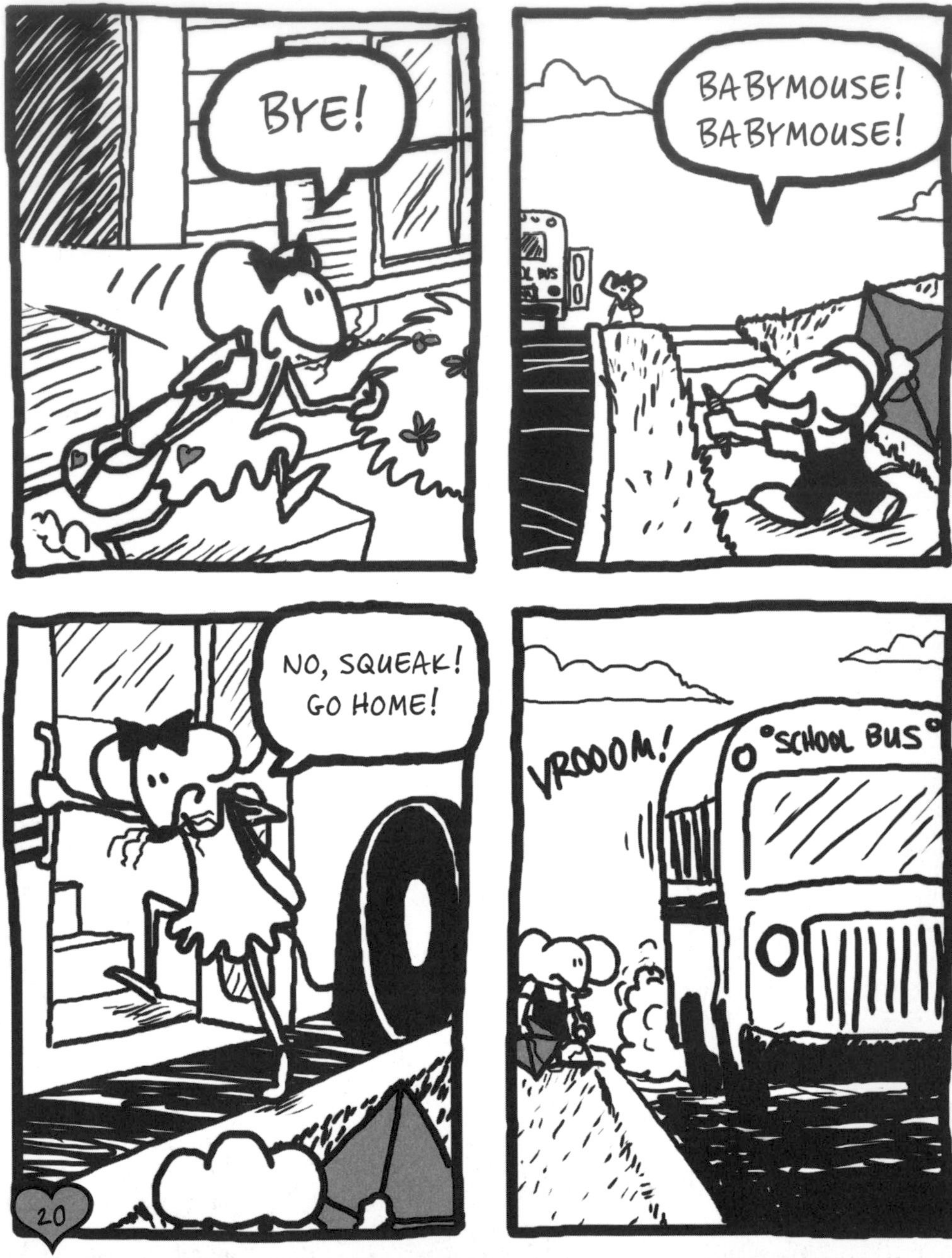
BYE!
BABYMOUSE! BABYMOUSE!
NO, SQUEAK! GO HOME!
VROOOM!
SCHOOL BUS

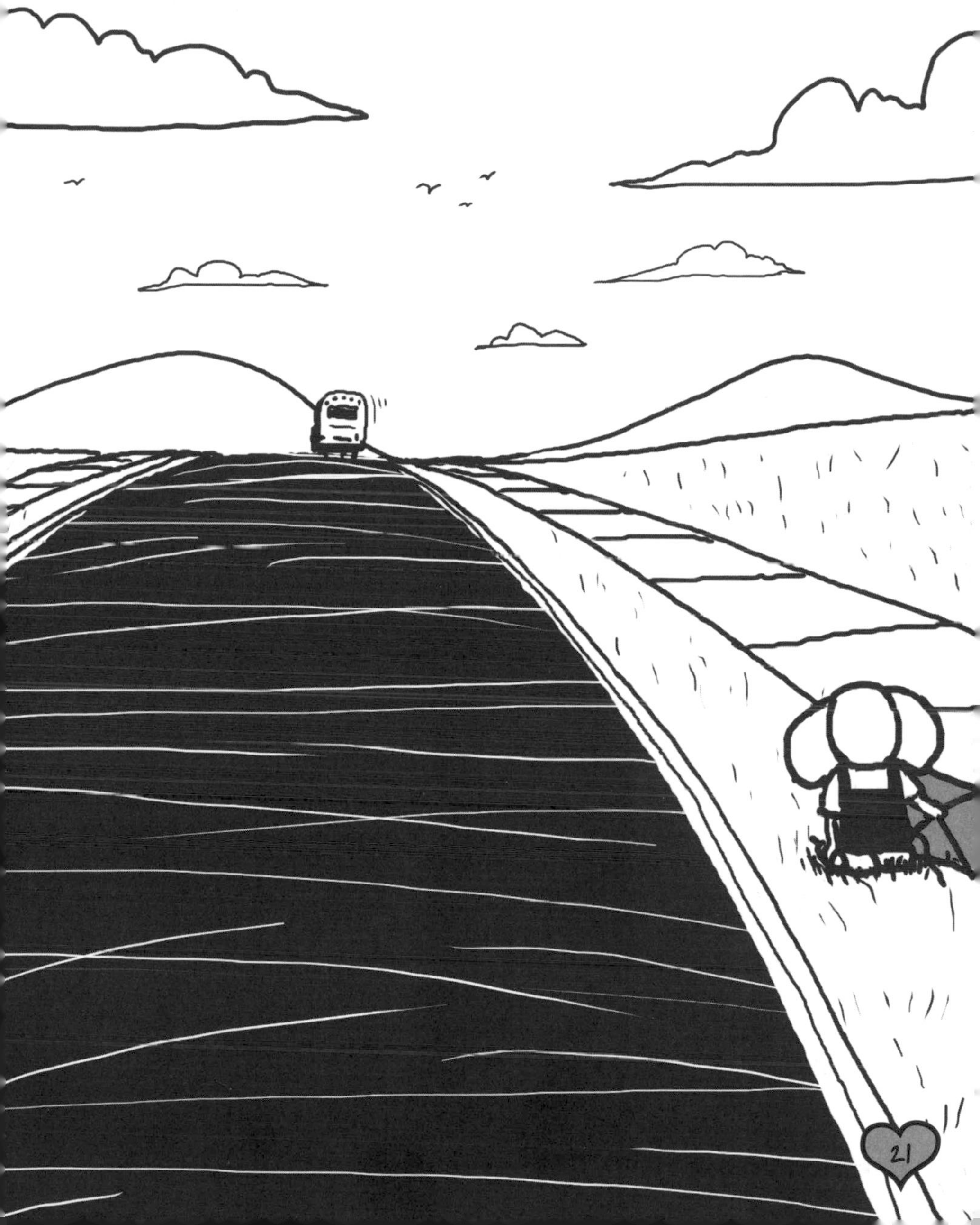

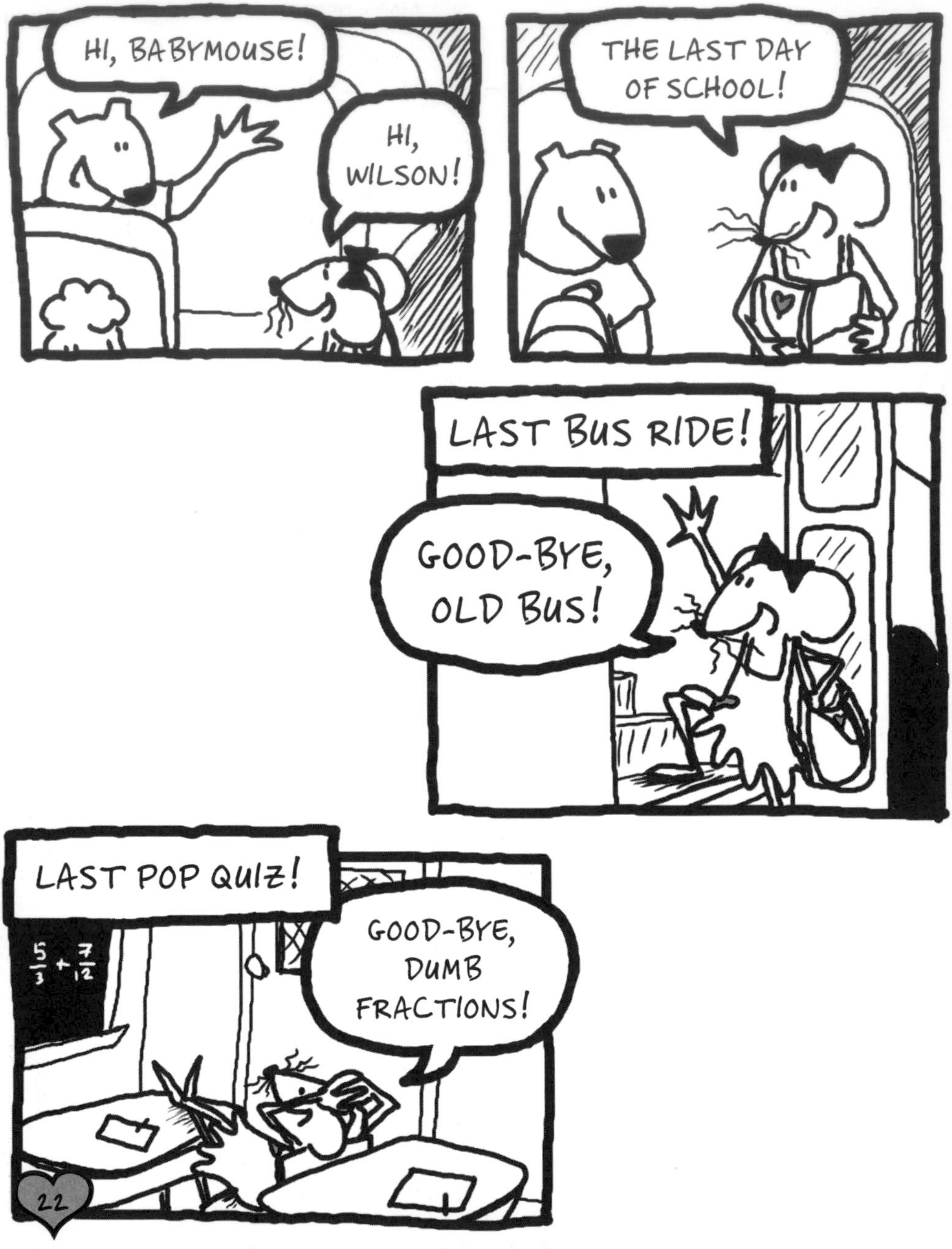
HI, BABYMOUSE!
HI, WILSON!
THE LAST DAY OF SCHOOL!
LAST BUS RIDE!
GOOD-BYE, OLD BUS!
LAST POP QUIZ!
$\frac{5}{3} + \frac{7}{12}$
GOOD-BYE, DUMB FRACTIONS!

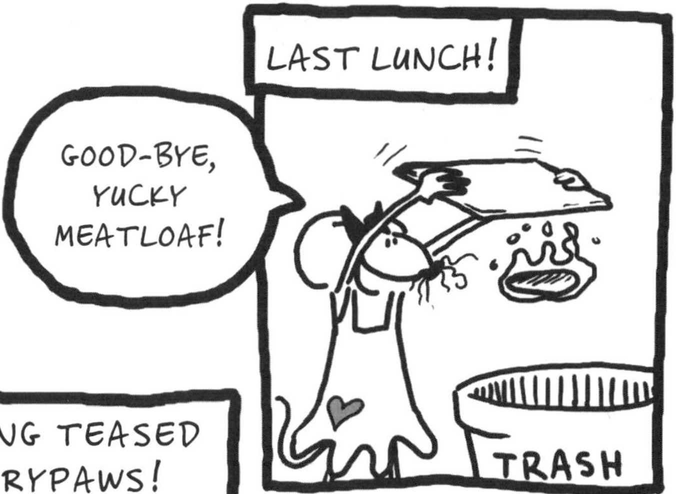
LAST LUNCH!
GOOD-BYE, YUCKY MEATLOAF!
TRASH

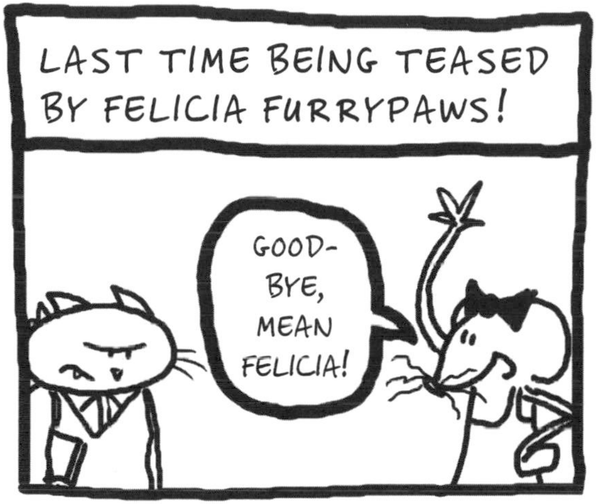
LAST TIME BEING TEASED BY FELICIA FURRYPAWS!
GOOD-BYE, MEAN FELICIA!

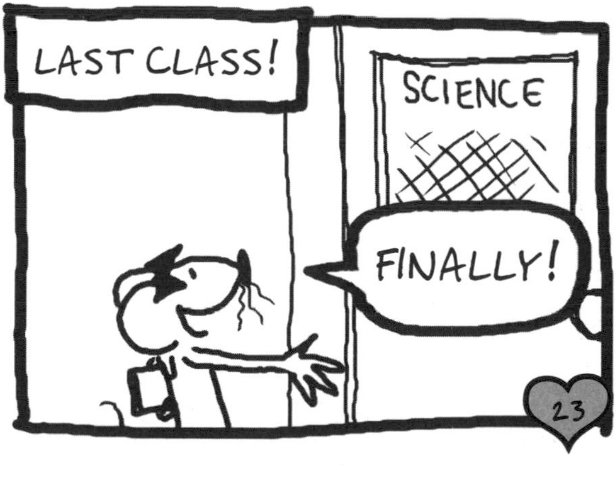
LAST CLASS!
SCIENCE
FINALLY!

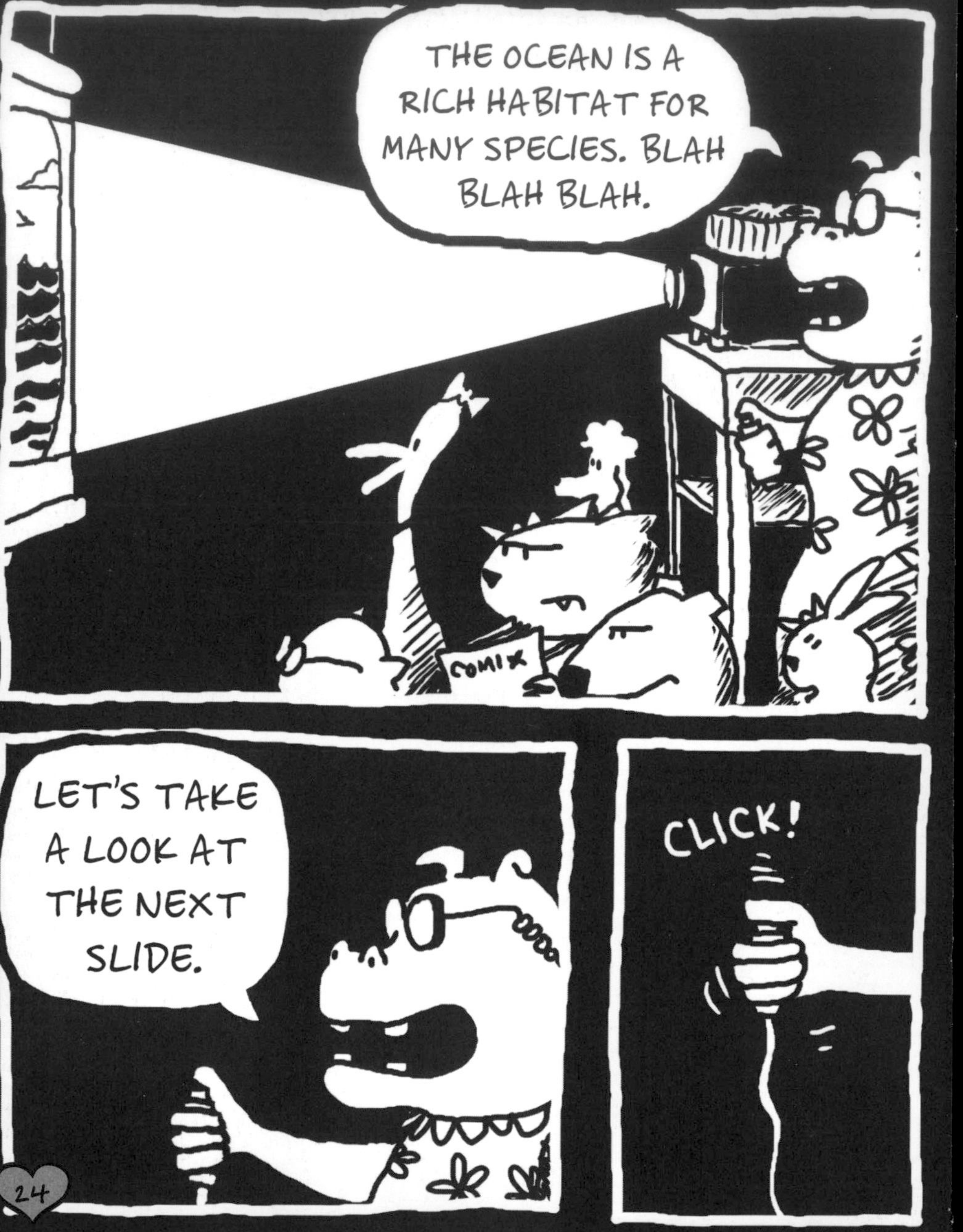
THE OCEAN IS A RICH HABITAT FOR MANY SPECIES. BLAH BLAH BLAH.
COMIX
LET'S TAKE A LOOK AT THE NEXT SLIDE.
CLICK!

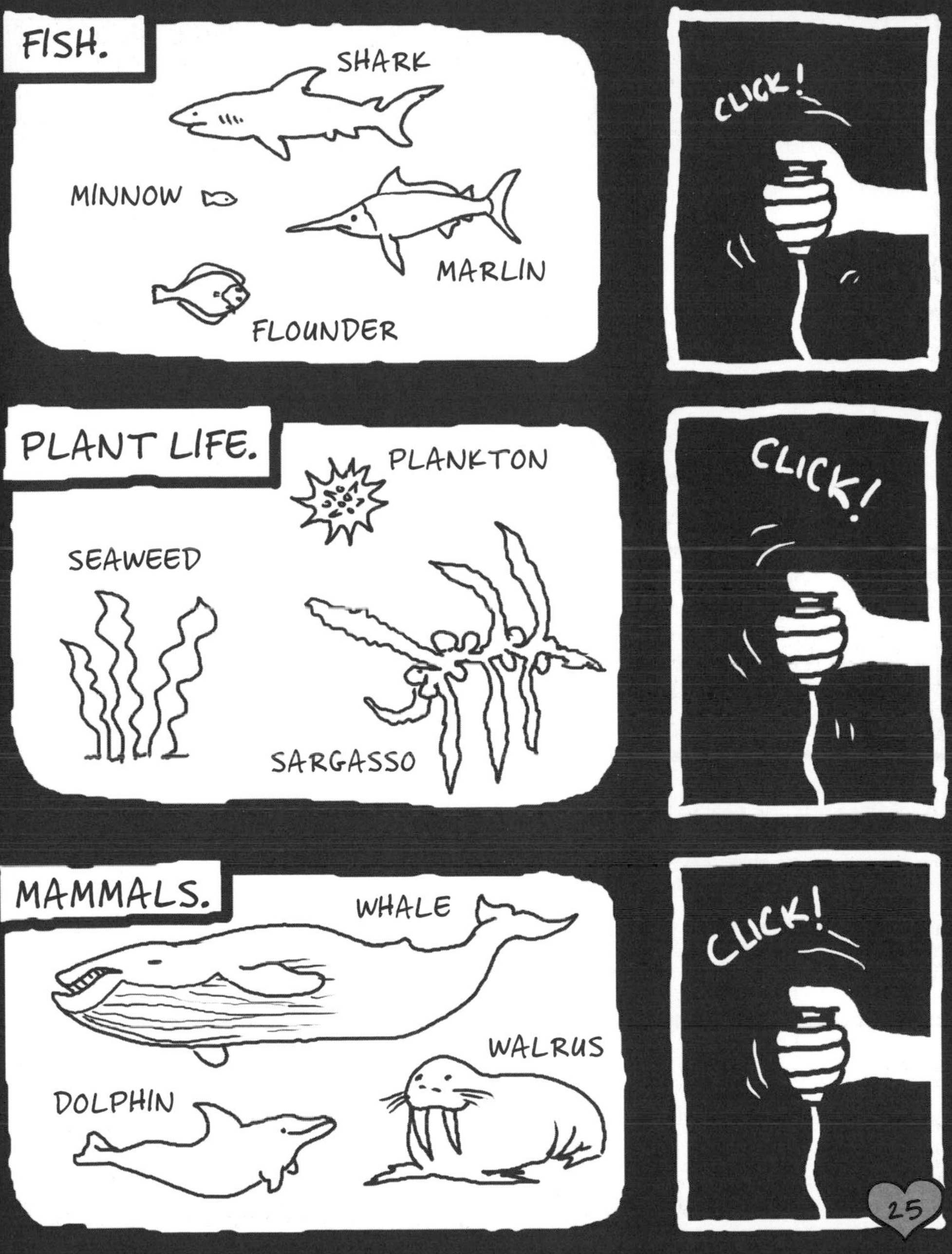
FISH.
SHARK
MINNOW
MARLIN
FLOUNDER
CLICK!
PLANT LIFE.
PLANKTON
SEAWEED
SARGASSO
CLICK!
MAMMALS.
WHALE
WALRUS
DOLPHIN
CLICK!

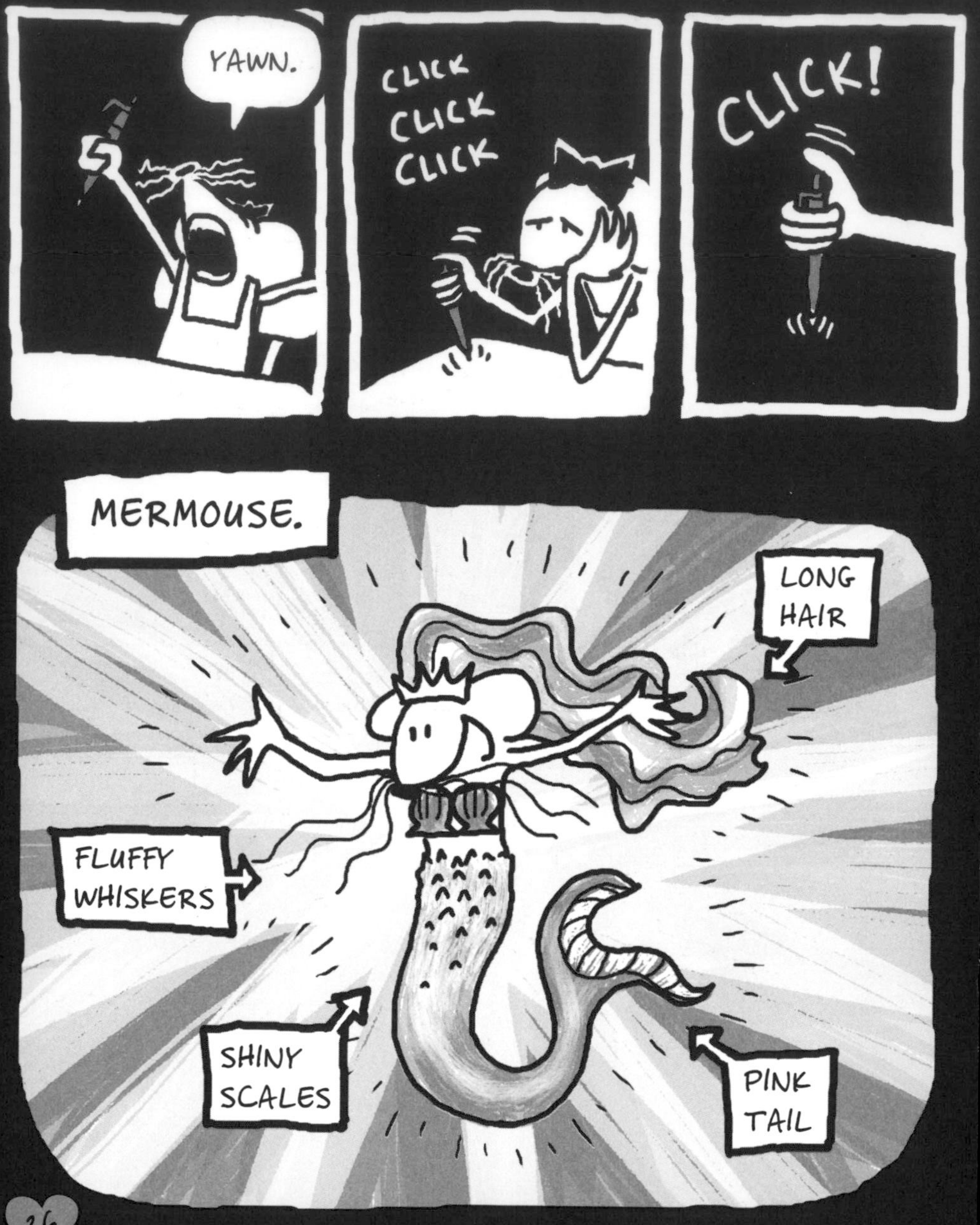
YAWN.
CLICK
CLICK
CLICK
CLICK!
MERMOUSE.
LONG HAIR
FLUFFY WHISKERS
SHINY SCALES
PINK TAIL

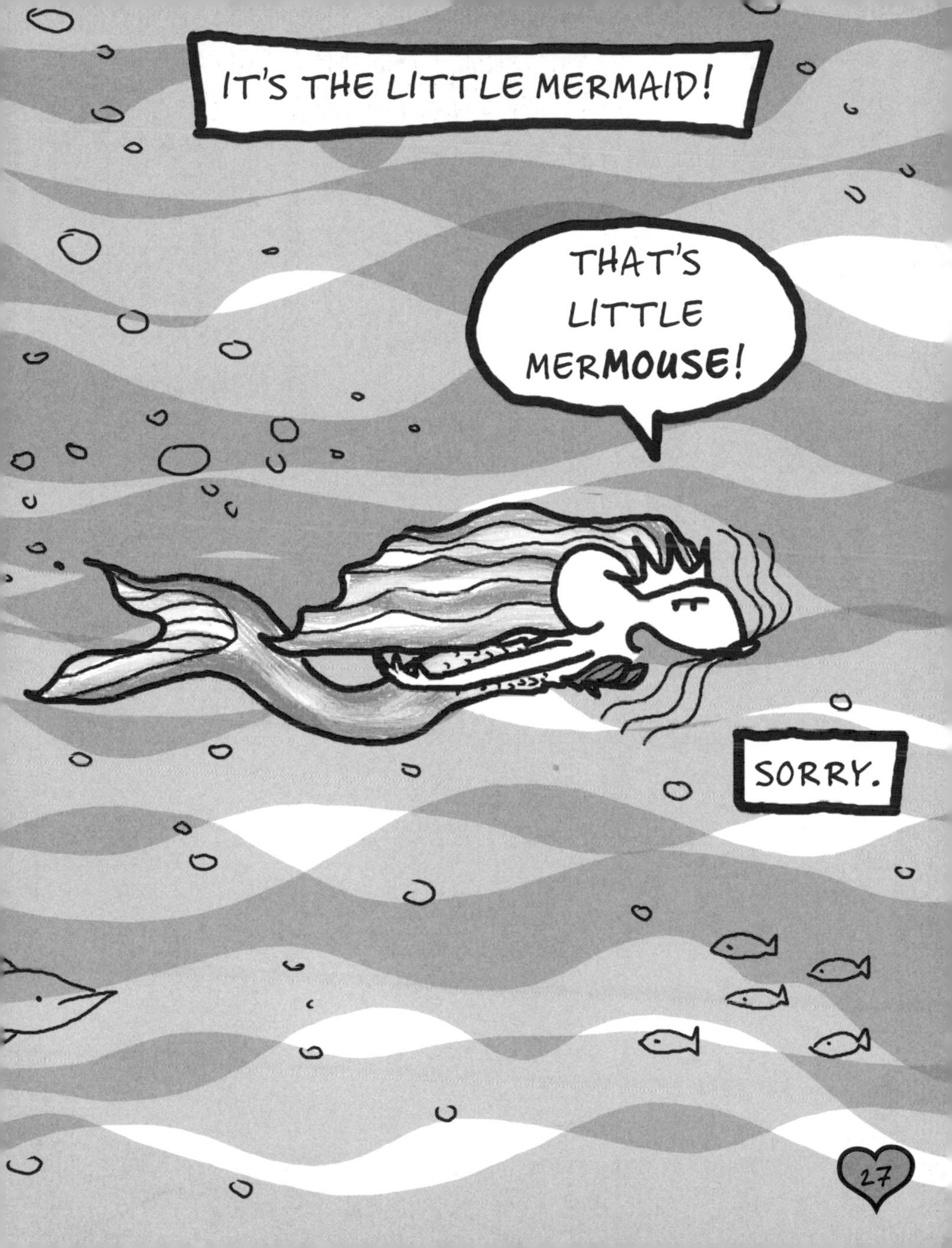
IT'S THE LITTLE MERMAID!
THAT'S LITTLE MERMOUSE!
SORRY.

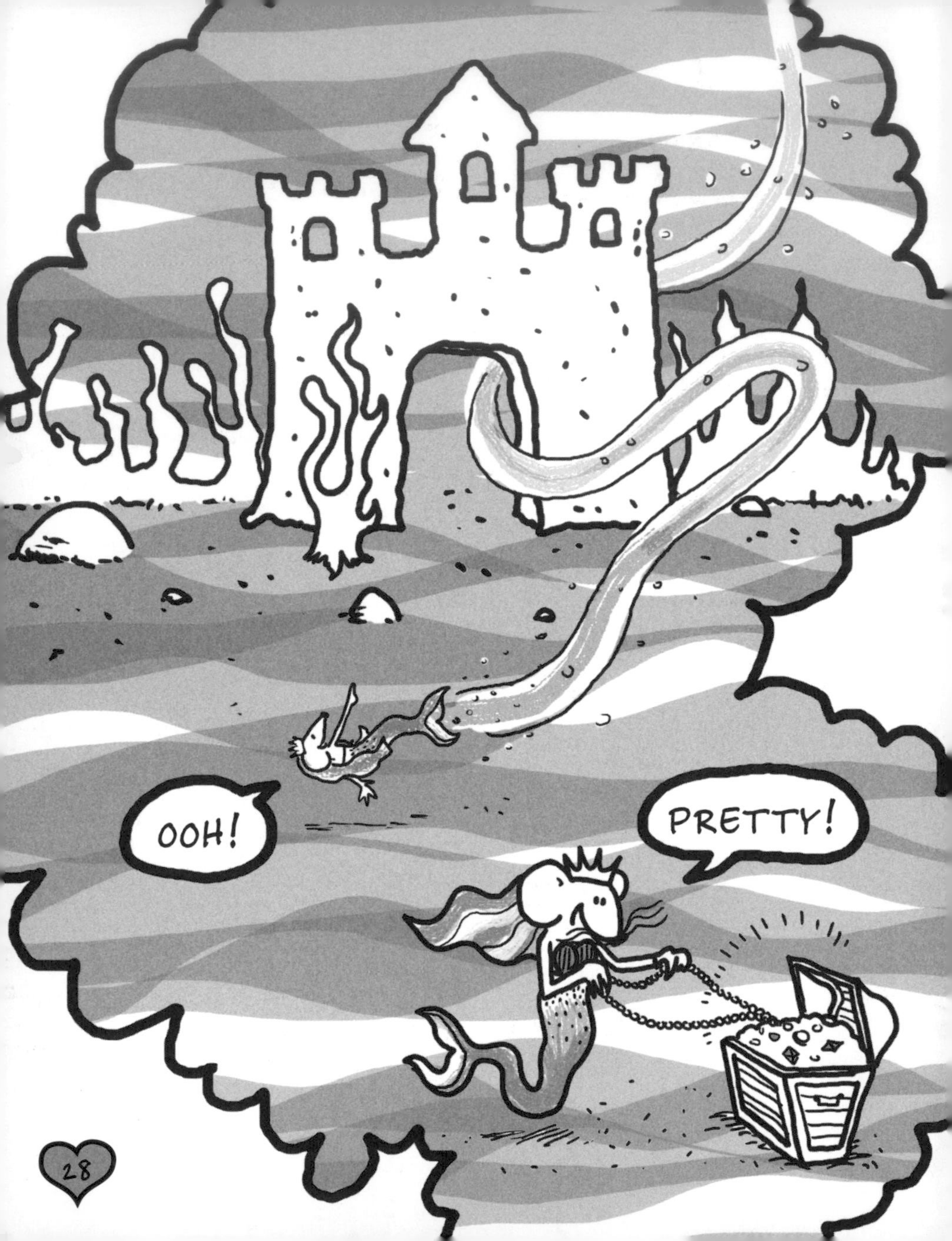
OOH!
PRETTY!

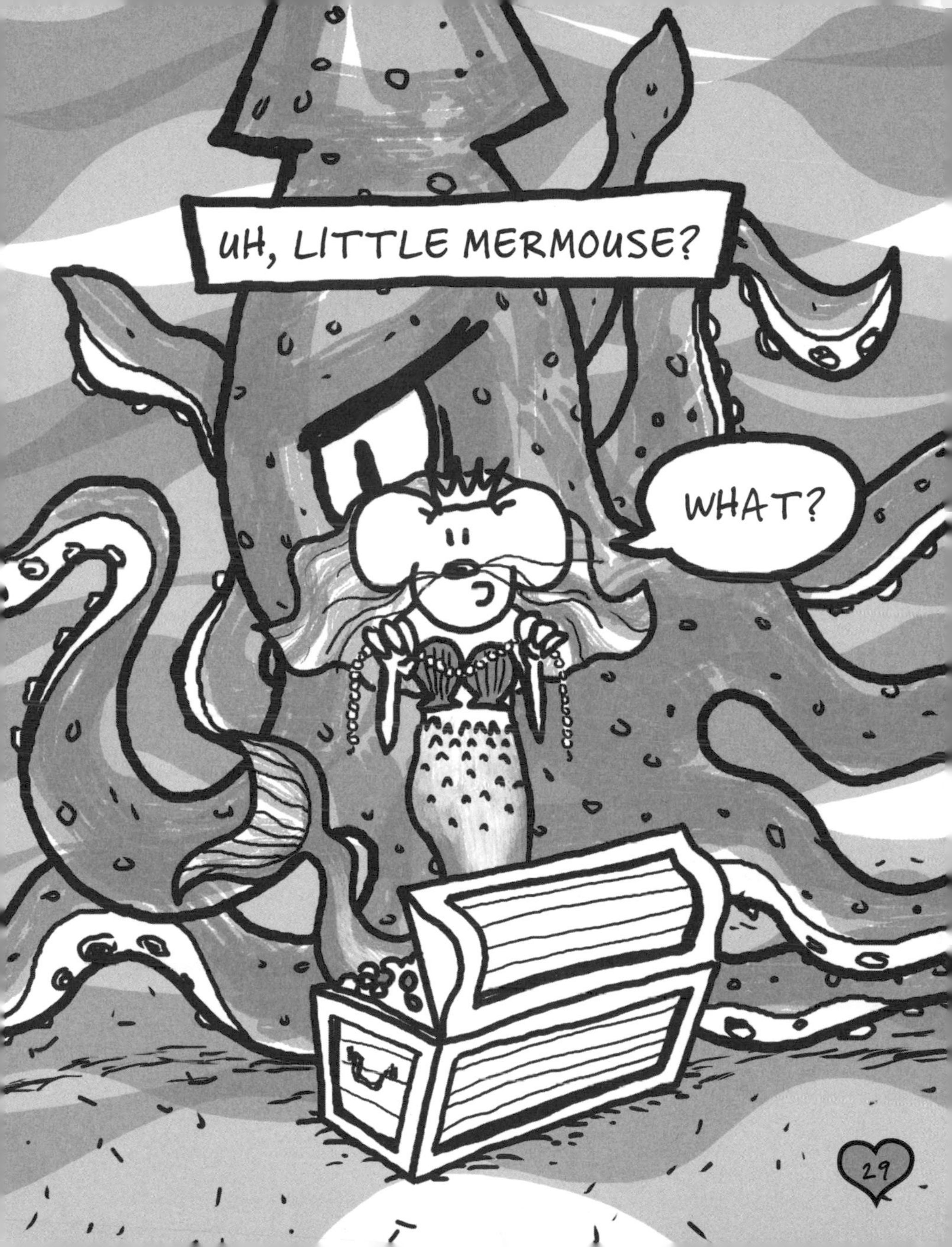
UH, LITTLE MERMOUSE?
WHAT?

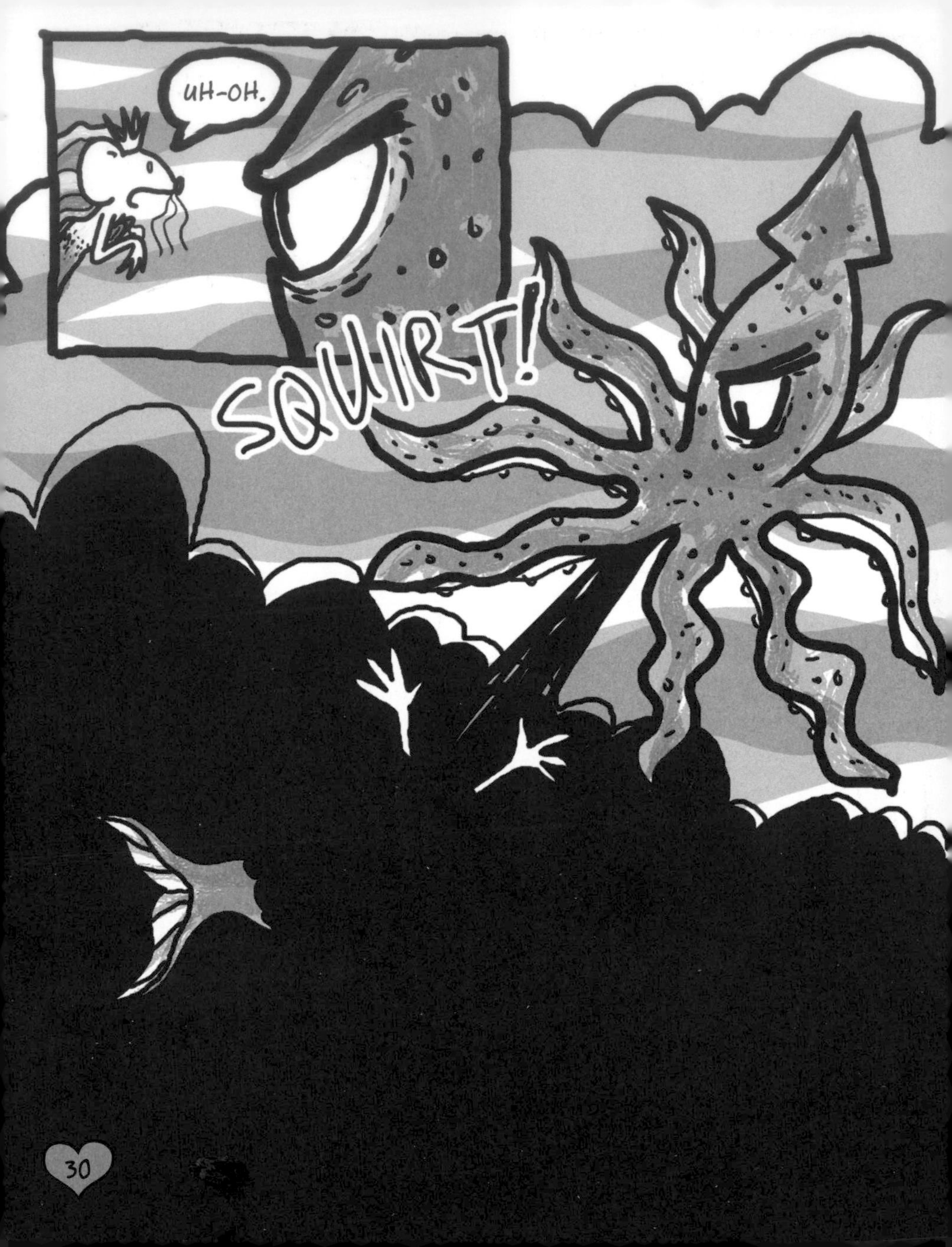
UH-OH.
SQUIRT!

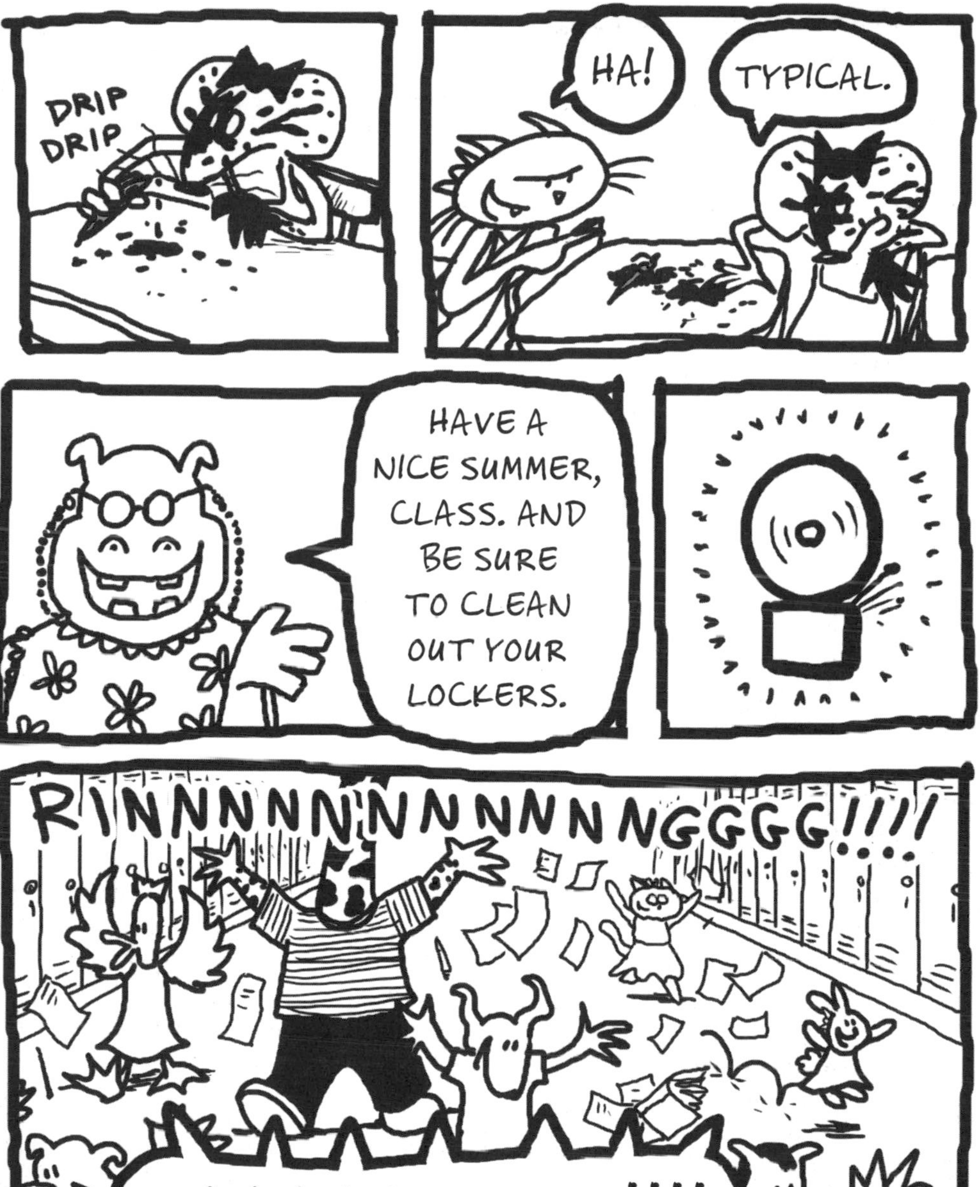
DRIP DRIP
HA!
TYPICAL.
HAVE A NICE SUMMER, CLASS. AND BE SURE TO CLEAN OUT YOUR LOCKERS.
RINNNNNNNNNNNNGGGG!!!!
YAAAAAYYYYYY!!!!

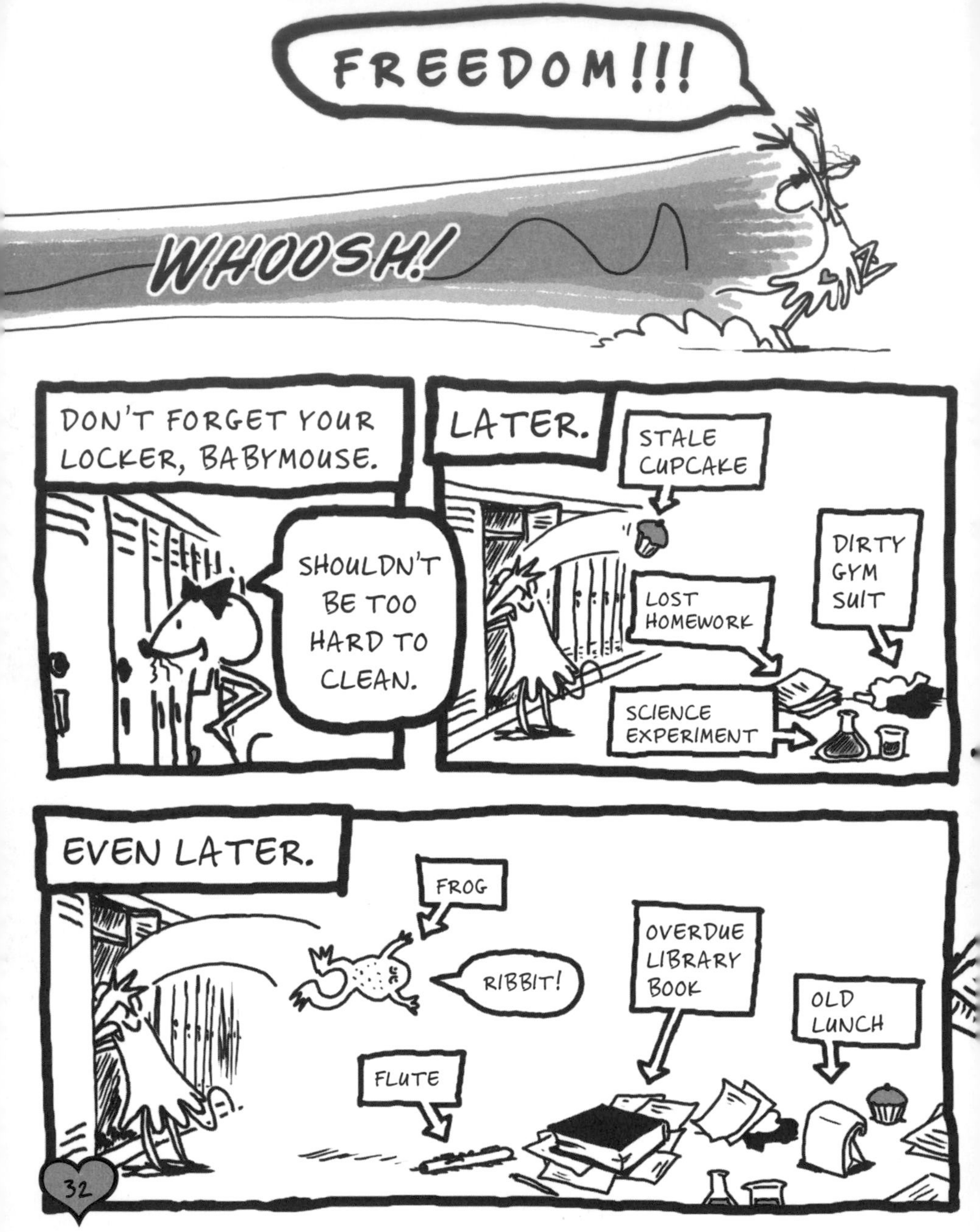
FREEDOM!!!
WHOOSH!
DON'T FORGET YOUR LOCKER, BABYMOUSE.
SHOULDN'T BE TOO HARD TO CLEAN.
LATER.
STALE CUPCAKE
DIRTY GYM SUIT
LOST HOMEWORK
SCIENCE EXPERIMENT
EVEN LATER.
FROG
RIBBIT!
OVERDUE LIBRARY BOOK
OLD LUNCH
FLUTE

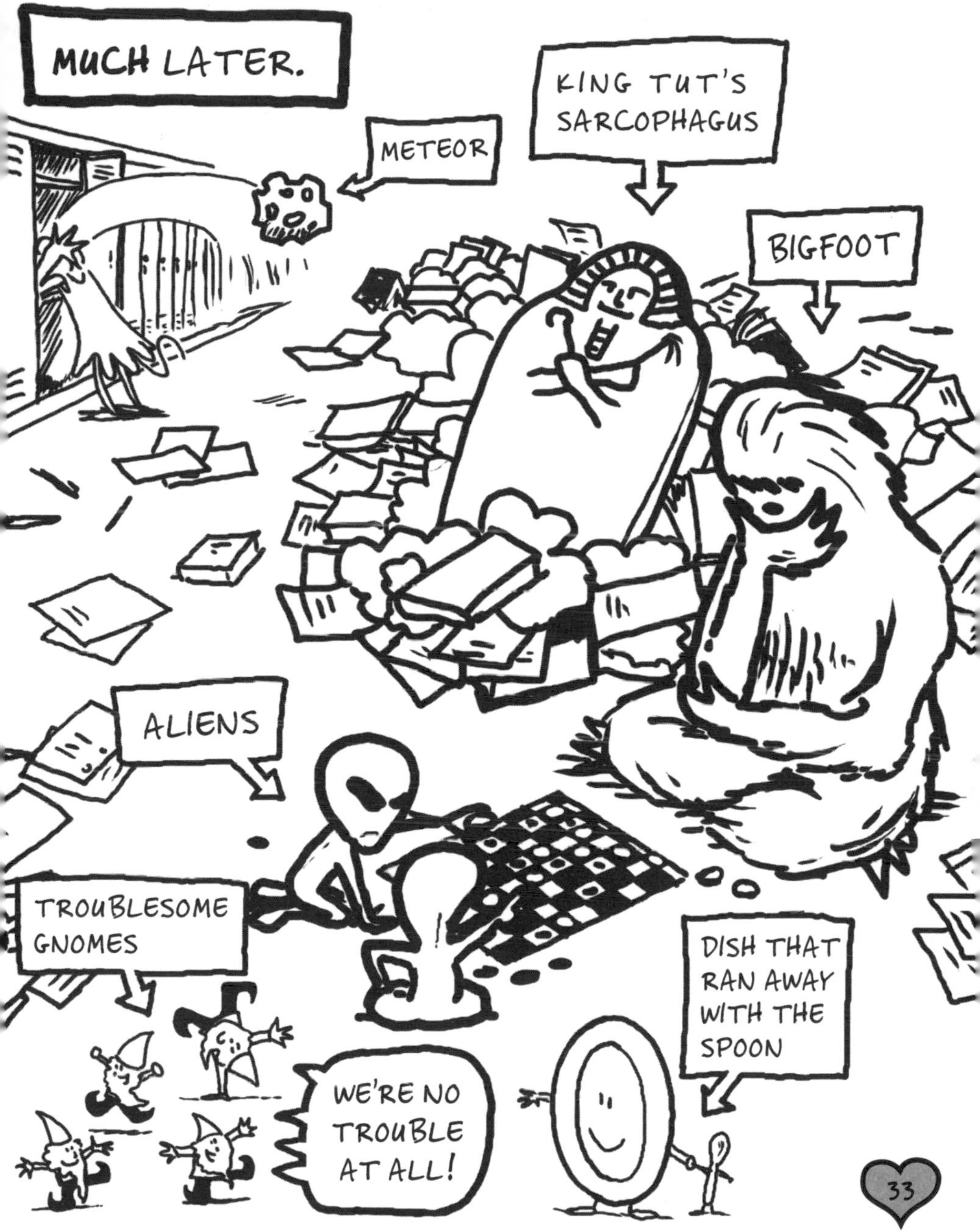
MUCH LATER.
METEOR
KING TUT'S SARCOPHAGUS
BIGFOOT
ALIENS
TROUBLESOME GNOMES
DISH THAT RAN AWAY WITH THE SPOON
WE'RE NO TROUBLE AT ALL!

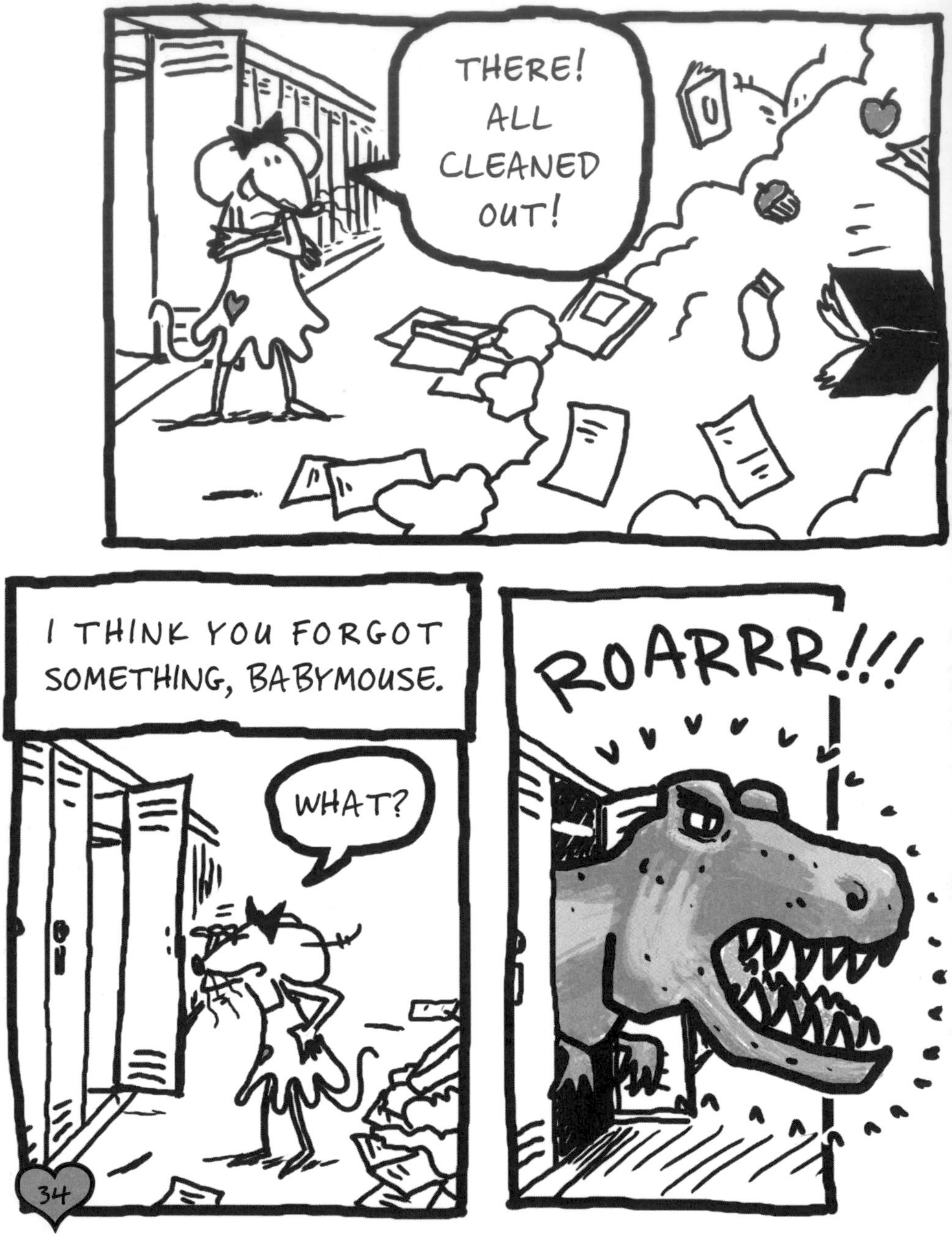
THERE! ALL CLEANED OUT!
I THINK YOU FORGOT SOMETHING, BABYMOUSE.
WHAT?
ROARRR!!!

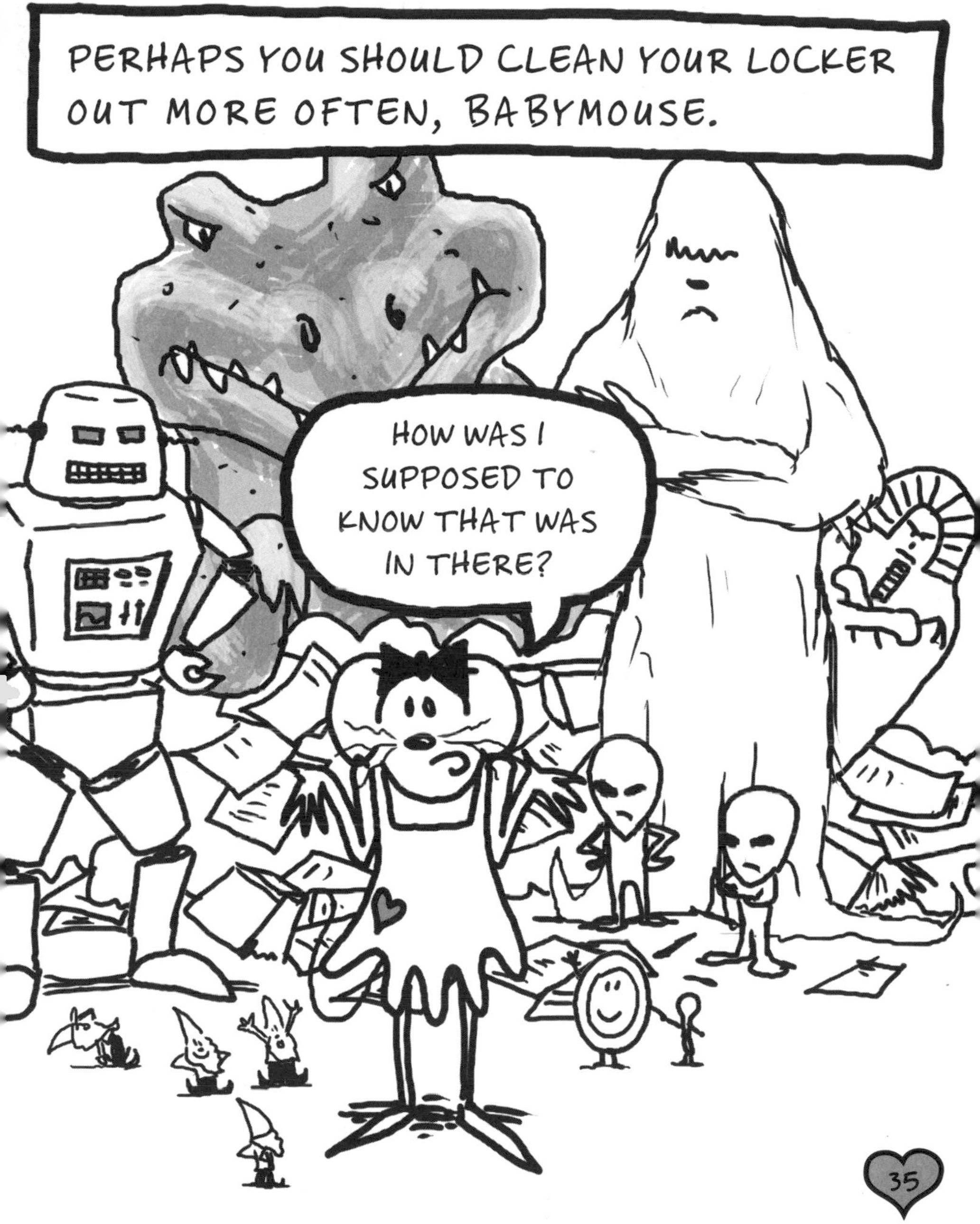
PERHAPS YOU SHOULD CLEAN YOUR LOCKER OUT MORE OFTEN, BABYMOUSE.
HOW WAS I SUPPOSED TO KNOW THAT WAS IN THERE?

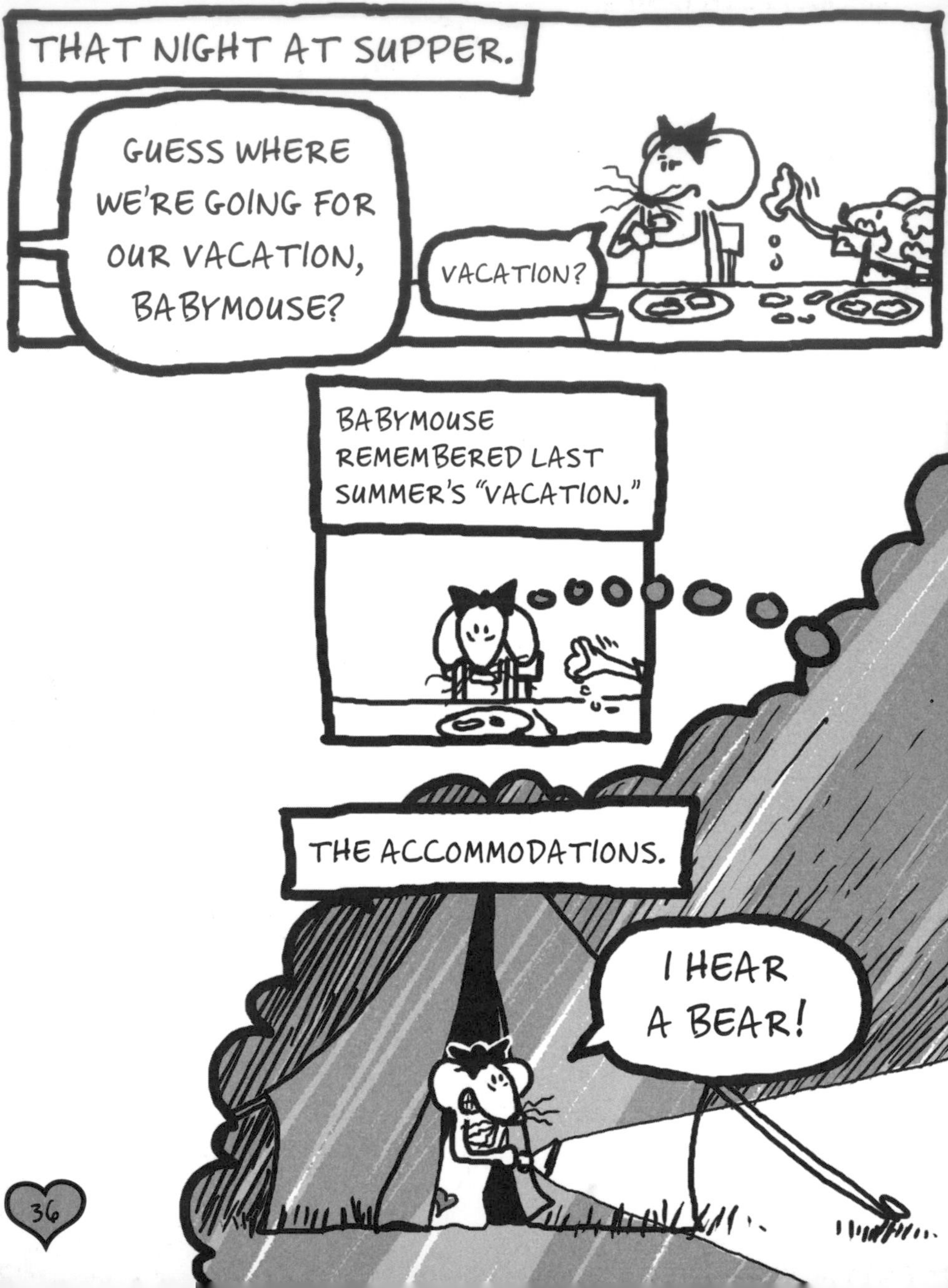
THAT NIGHT AT SUPPER.
GUESS WHERE WE'RE GOING FOR OUR VACATION, BABYMOUSE?
VACATION?
BABYMOUSE REMEMBERED LAST SUMMER'S "VACATION."
THE ACCOMMODATIONS.
I HEAR A BEAR!

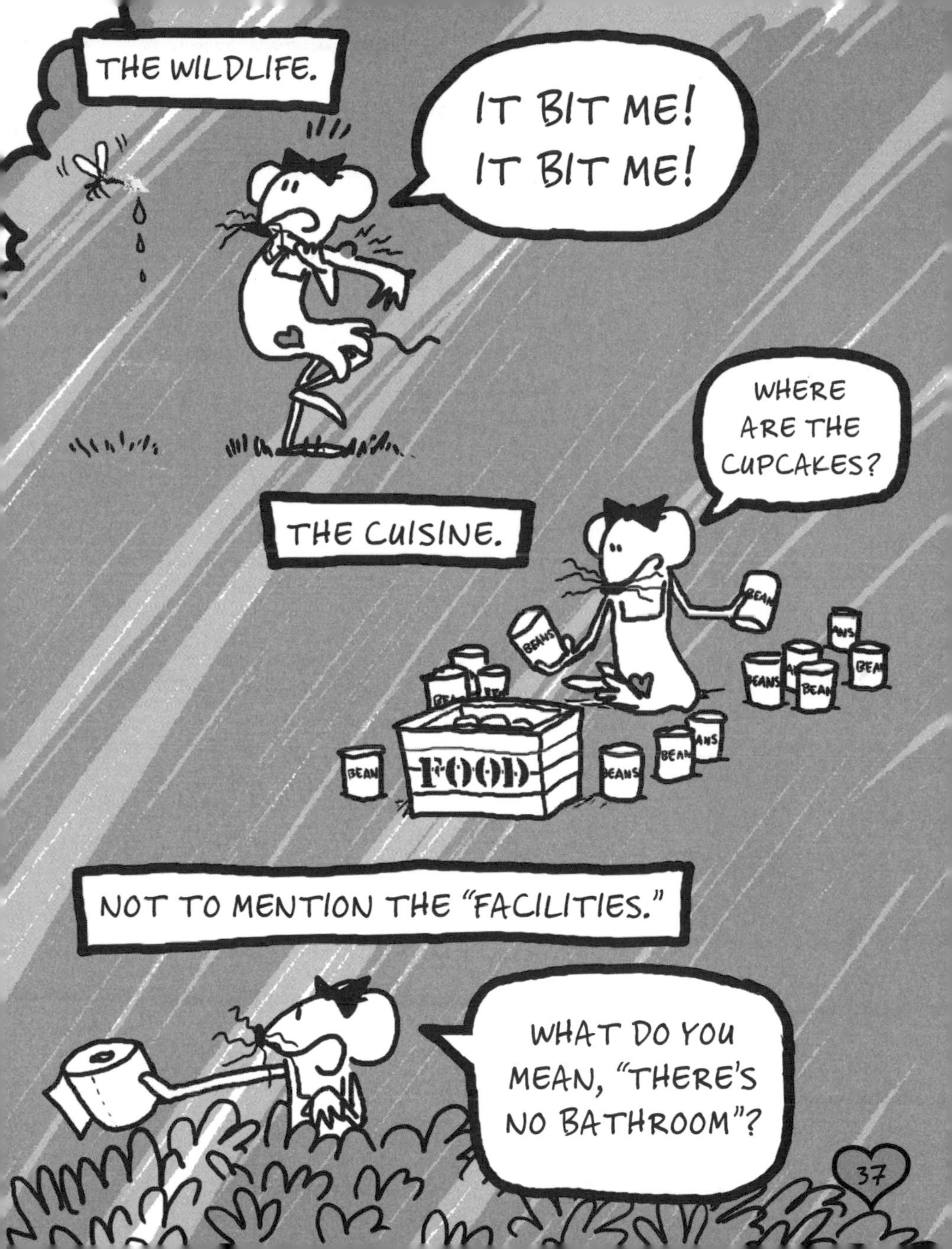
THE WILDLIFE.
IT BIT ME! IT BIT ME!
THE CUISINE.
WHERE ARE THE CUPCAKES?
FOOD
NOT TO MENTION THE "FACILITIES."
WHAT DO YOU MEAN, "THERE'S NO BATHROOM"?

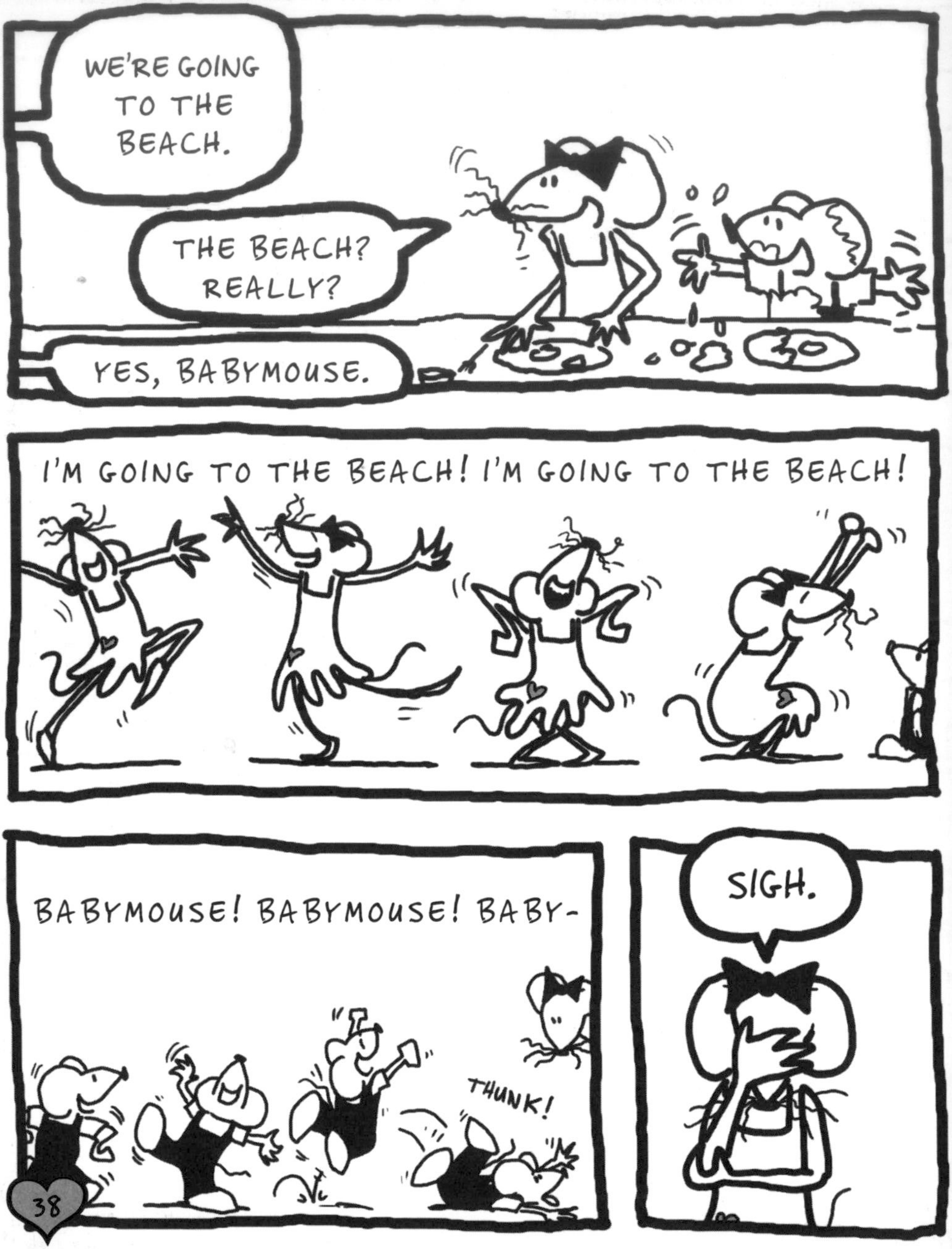
WE'RE GOING TO THE BEACH.
THE BEACH? REALLY?
YES, BABYMOUSE.
I'M GOING TO THE BEACH! I'M GOING TO THE BEACH!
BABYMOUSE! BABYMOUSE! BABY-
THUNK!
SIGH.

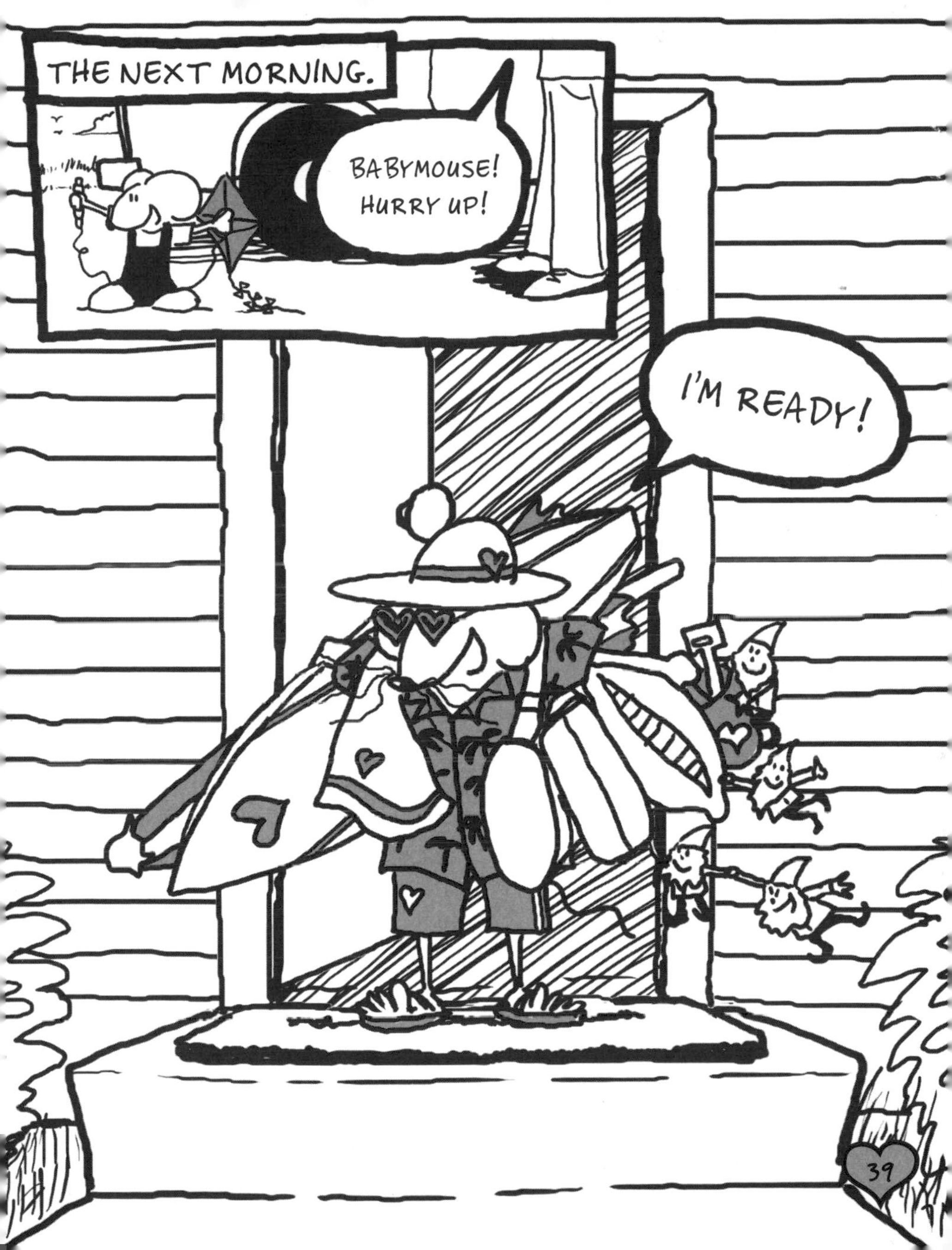
THE NEXT MORNING.
BABYMOUSE! HURRY UP!
I'M READY!

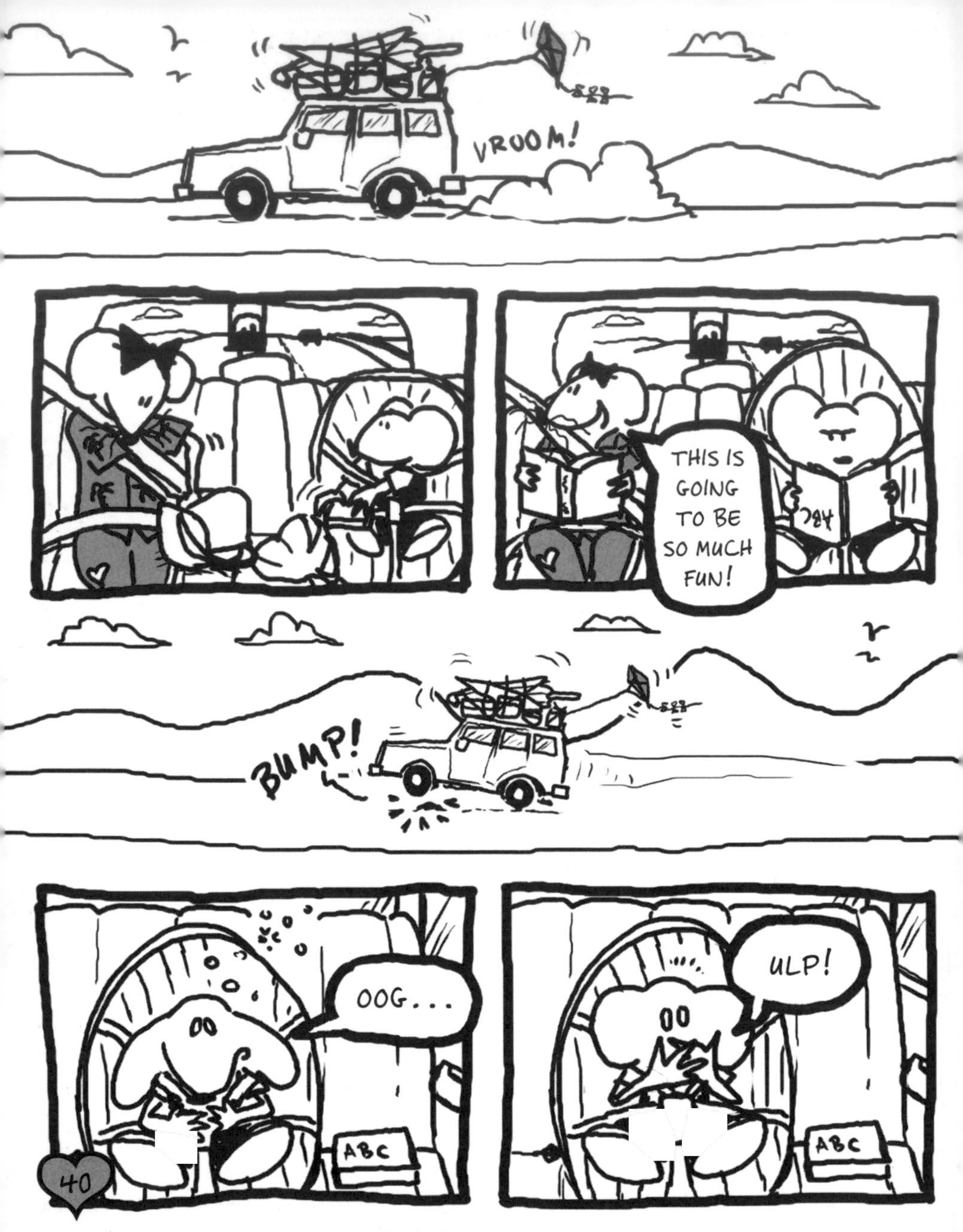
VROOM!
THIS IS GOING TO BE SO MUCH FUN!
BUMP!
OOG....
ULP!
ABC
ABC

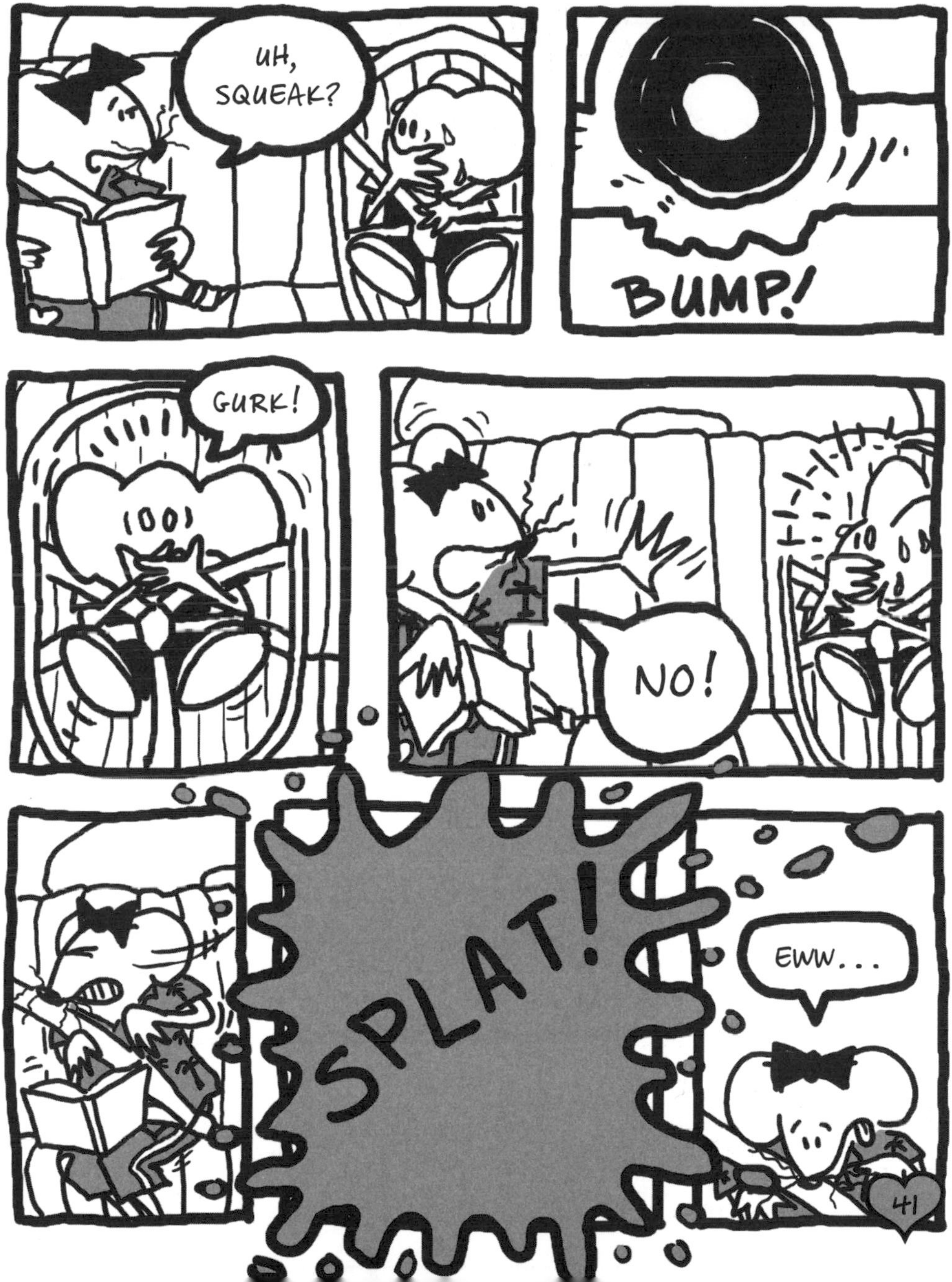
UH, SQUEAK?
BUMP!
GURK!
NO!
SPLAT!
EWW...
41

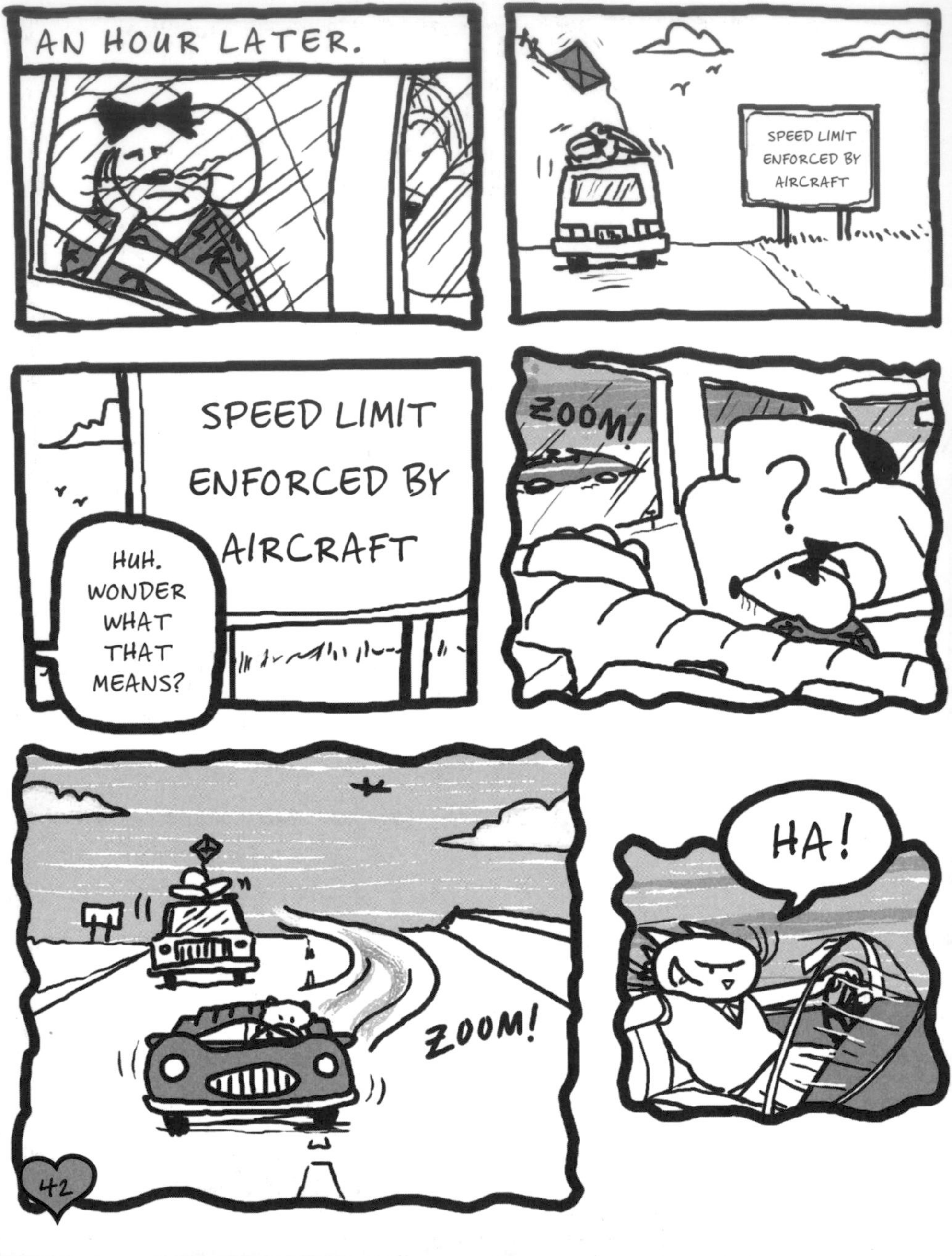
AN HOUR LATER.
SPEED LIMIT ENFORCED BY AIRCRAFT
SPEED LIMIT ENFORCED BY AIRCRAFT
HUH. WONDER WHAT THAT MEANS?
ZOOM!
ZOOM!
HA!

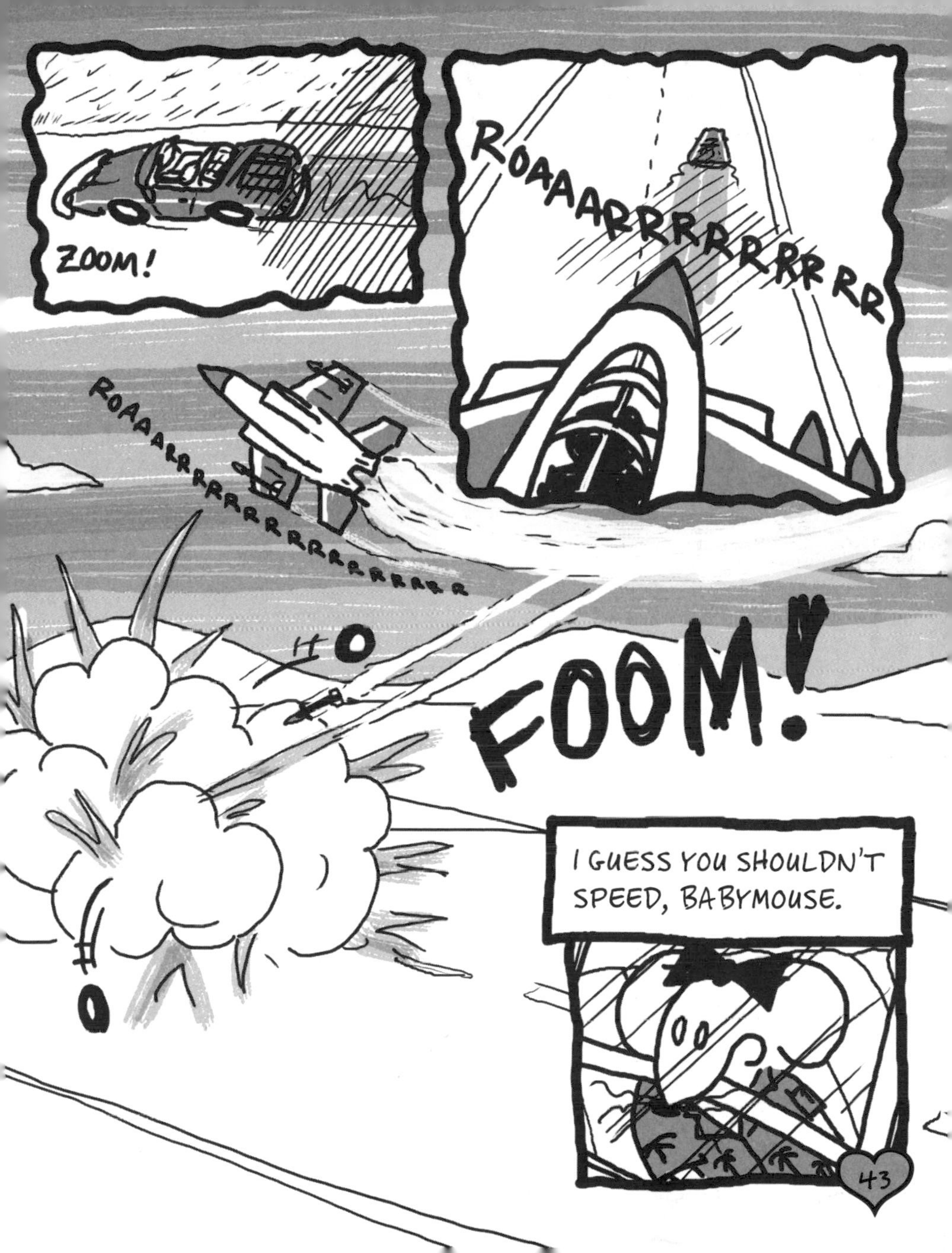
ZOOM!
ROAAAARRRRRRRRRRRRR
ROAAAARRRRRRRRRRRRRRRRRRRRR
FOOM!
I GUESS YOU SHOULDN'T SPEED, BABYMOUSE.

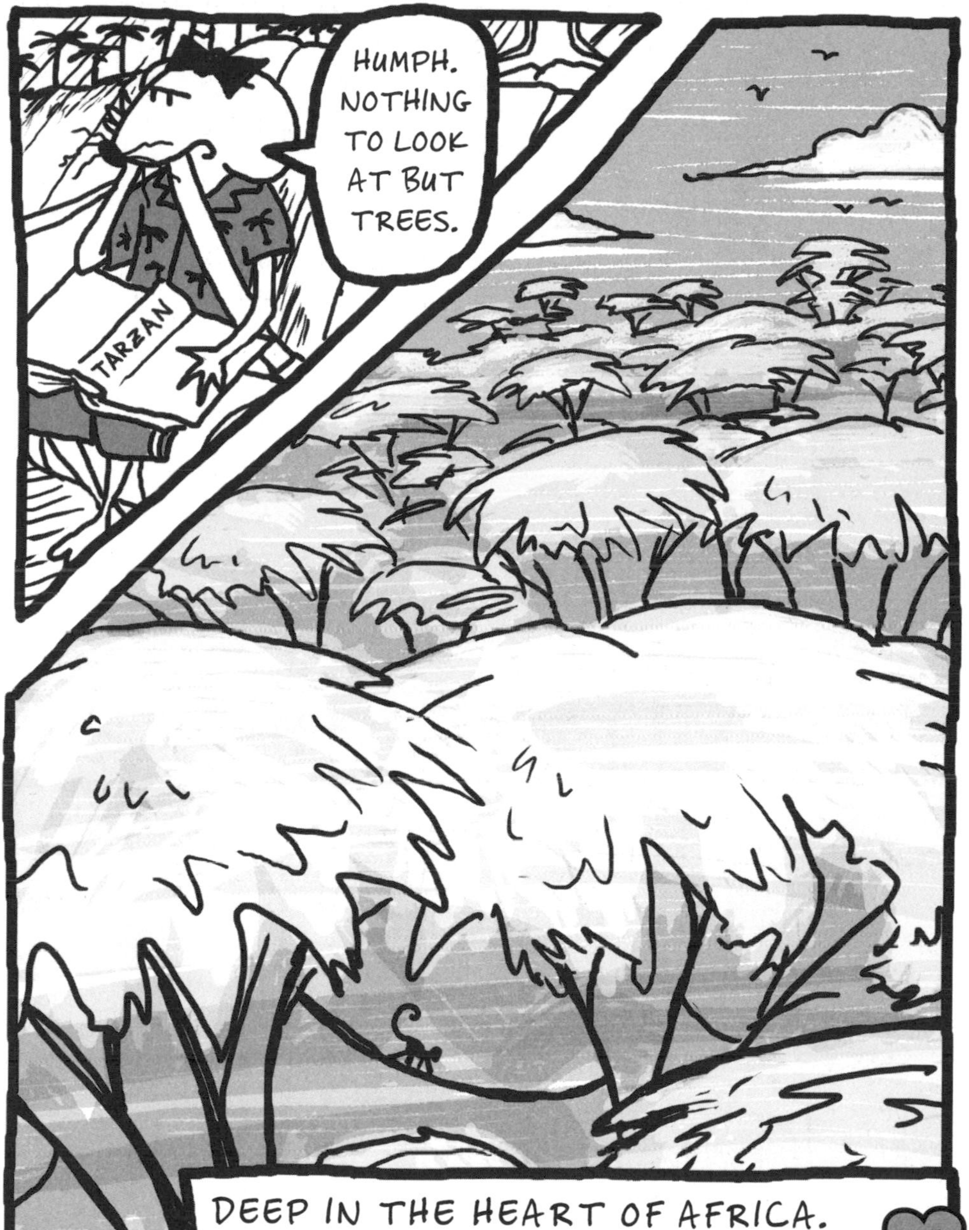
HUMPH. NOTHING TO LOOK AT BUT TREES.
TARZAN
DEEP IN THE HEART OF AFRICA.

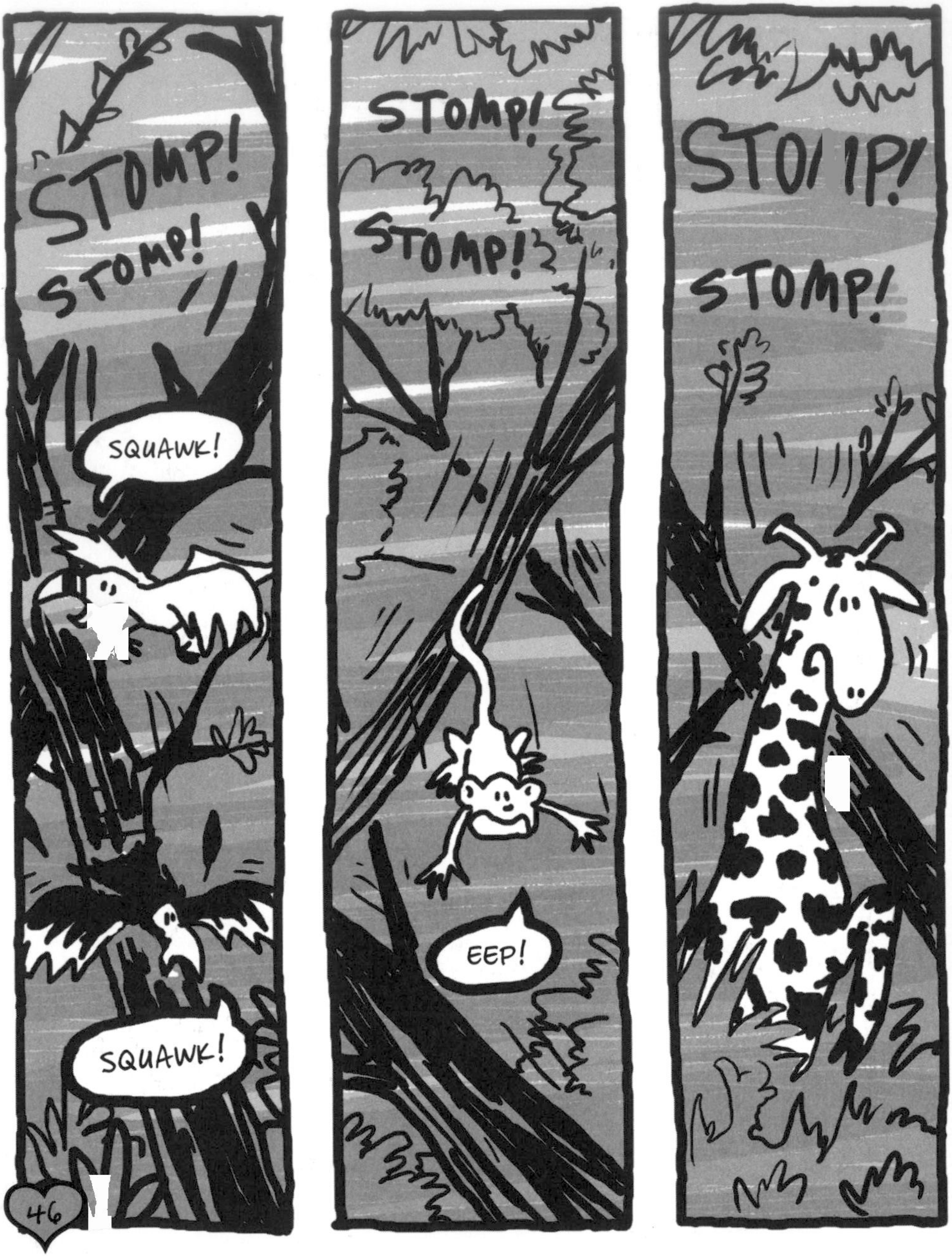
STOMP!
STOMP!
SQUAWK!
SQUAWK!
STOMP!
STOMP!
EEP!
STOMP!
STOMP!

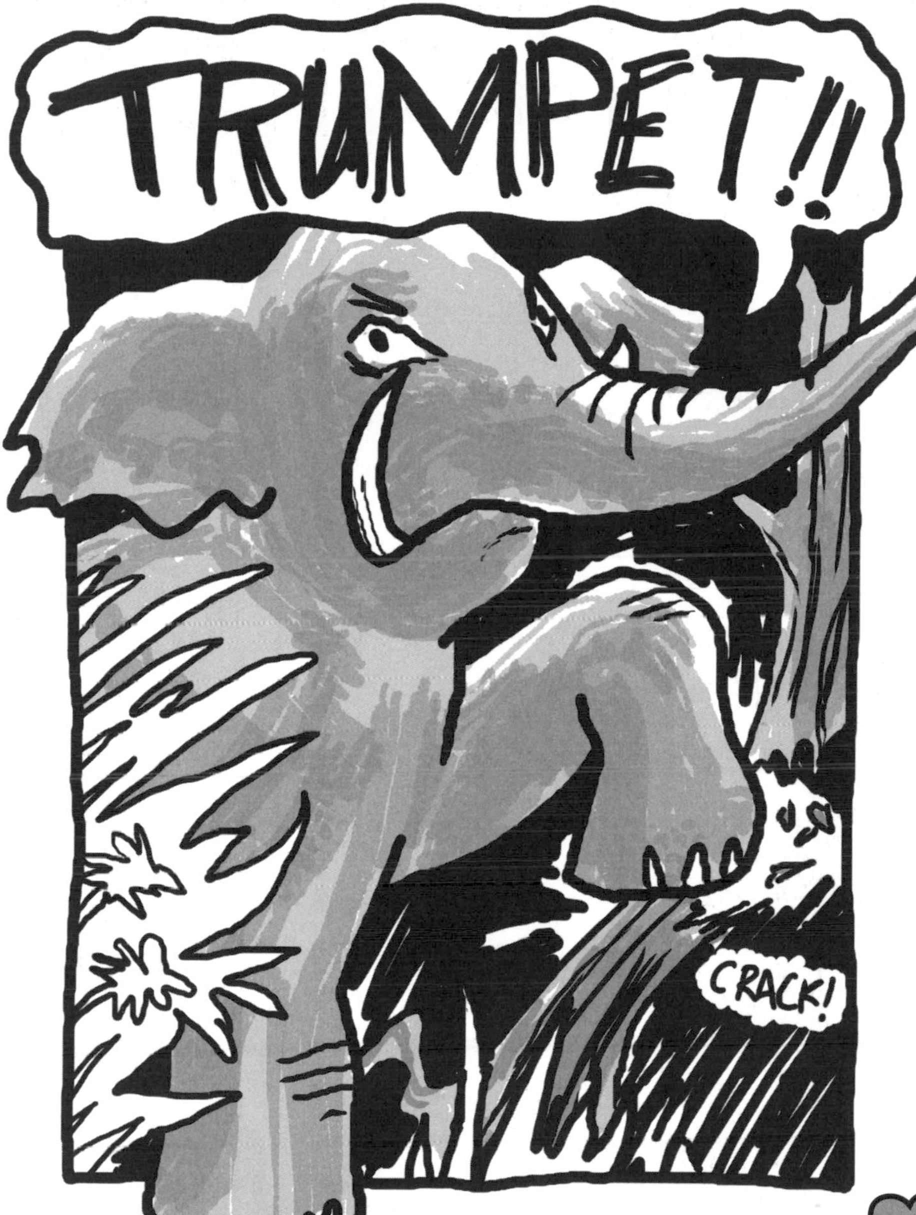
TRUMPET!!
CRACK!

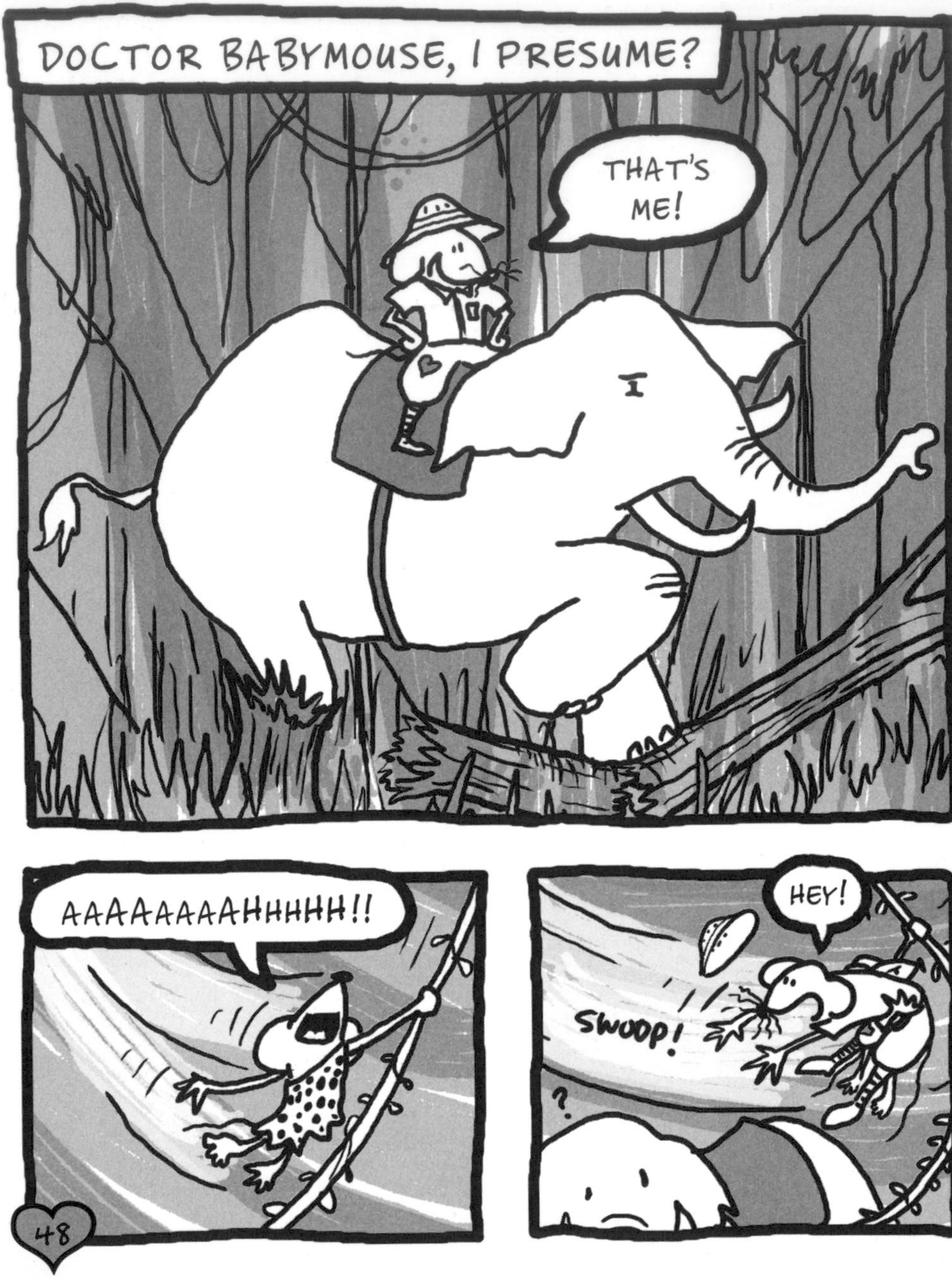
DOCTOR BABYMOUSE, I PRESUME?
THAT'S ME!
AAAAAAAAHHHHH!!
HEY!
SWOOP!
?

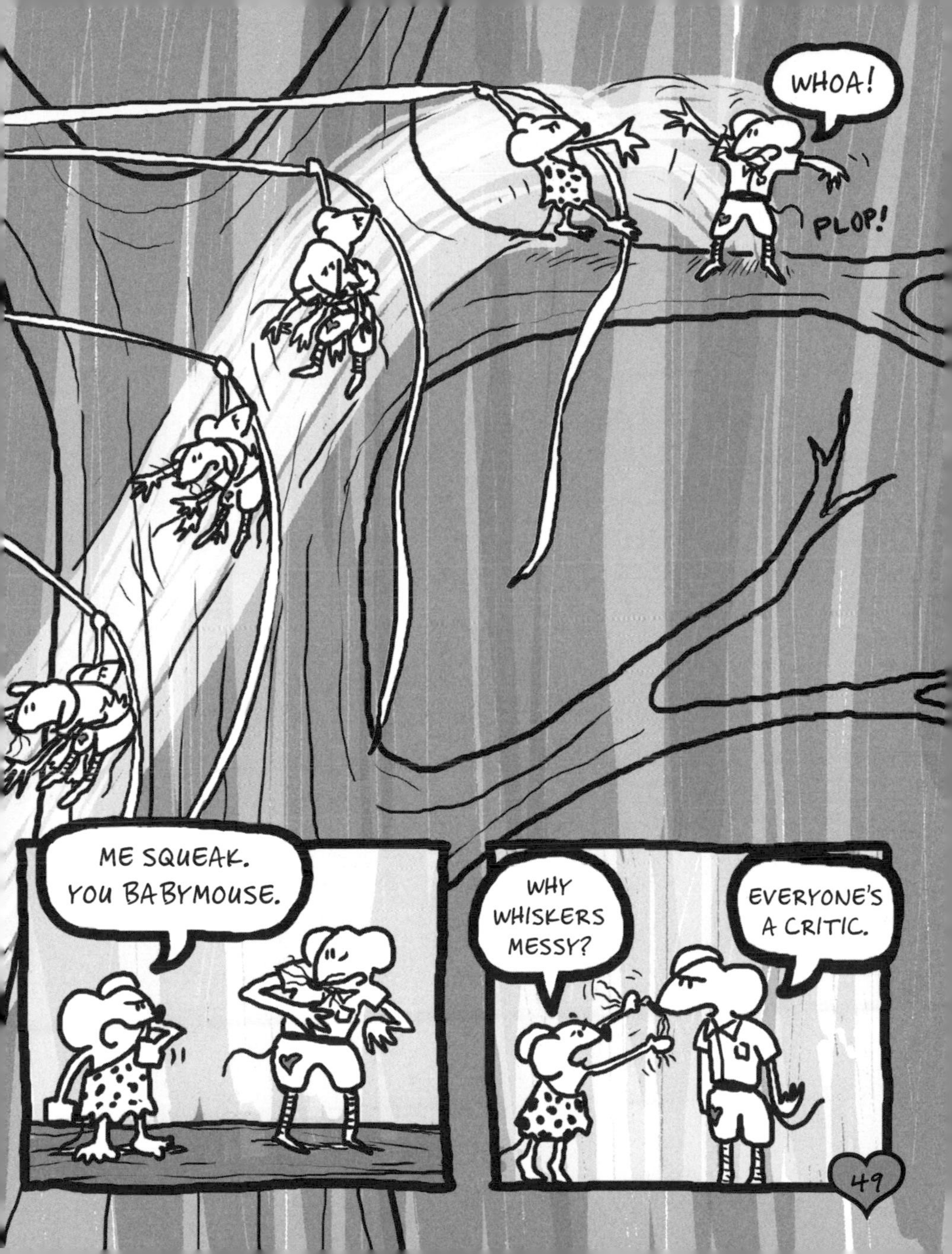
WHOA!
PLOP!
ME SQUEAK. YOU BABYMOUSE.
WHY WHISKERS MESSY?
EVERYONE'S A CRITIC.

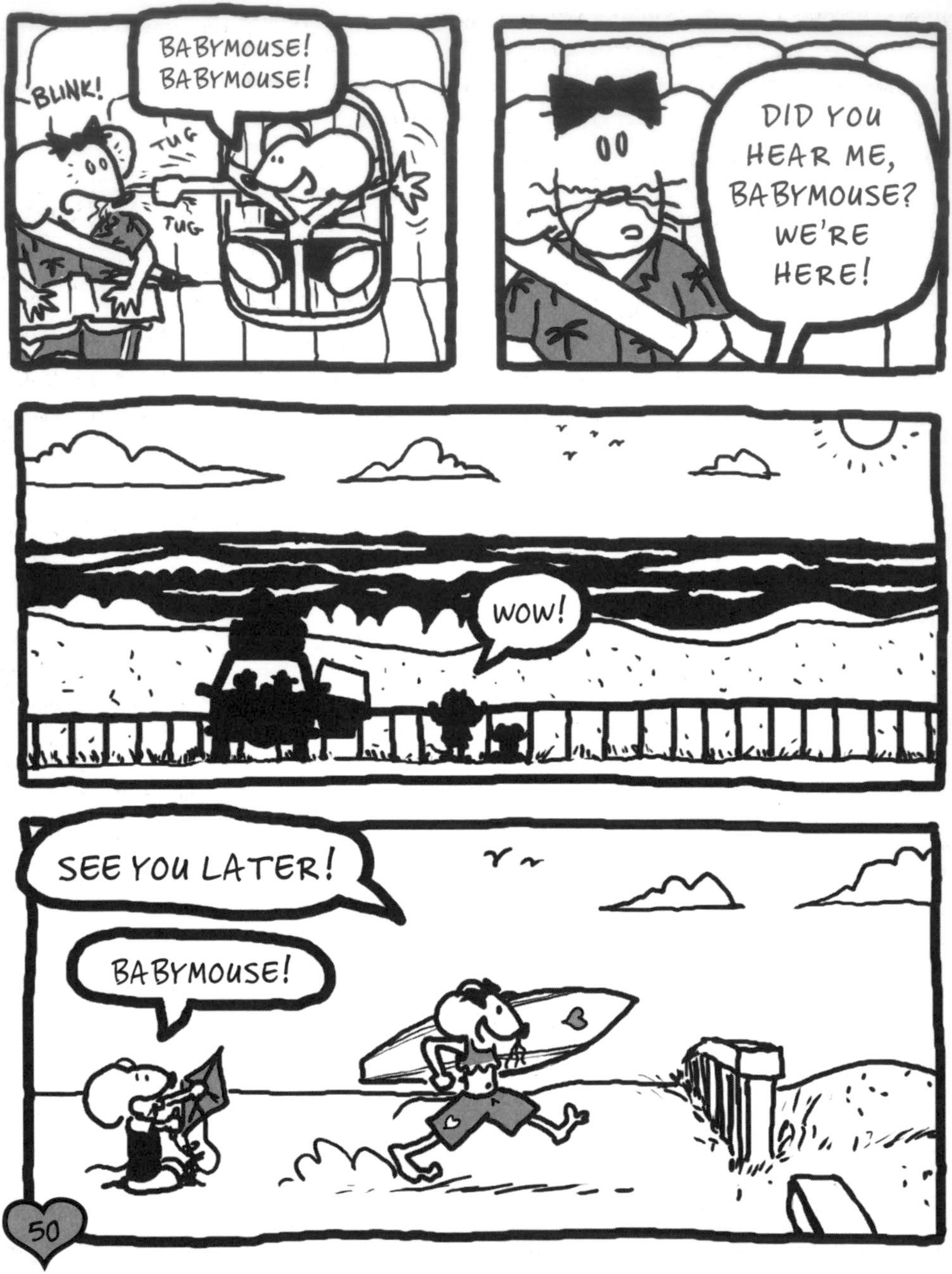
BLINK!
BABYMOUSE! BABYMOUSE!
TUG
TUG
DID YOU HEAR ME, BABYMOUSE? WE'RE HERE!
WOW!
SEE YOU LATER!
BABYMOUSE!

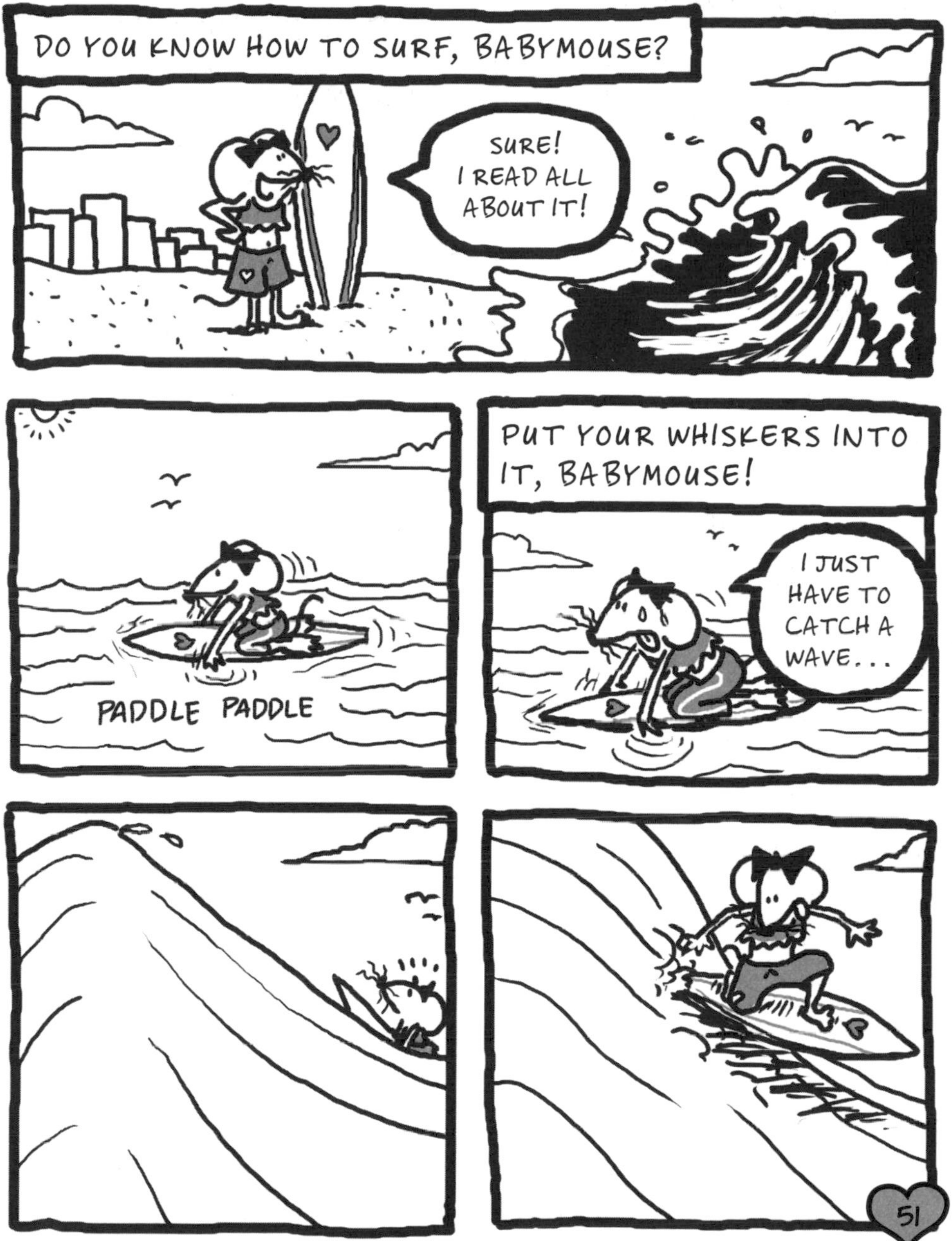
DO YOU KNOW HOW TO SURF, BABYMOUSE?
SURE! I READ ALL ABOUT IT!
PADDLE PADDLE
PUT YOUR WHISKERS INTO IT, BABYMOUSE!
I JUST HAVE TO CATCH A WAVE...

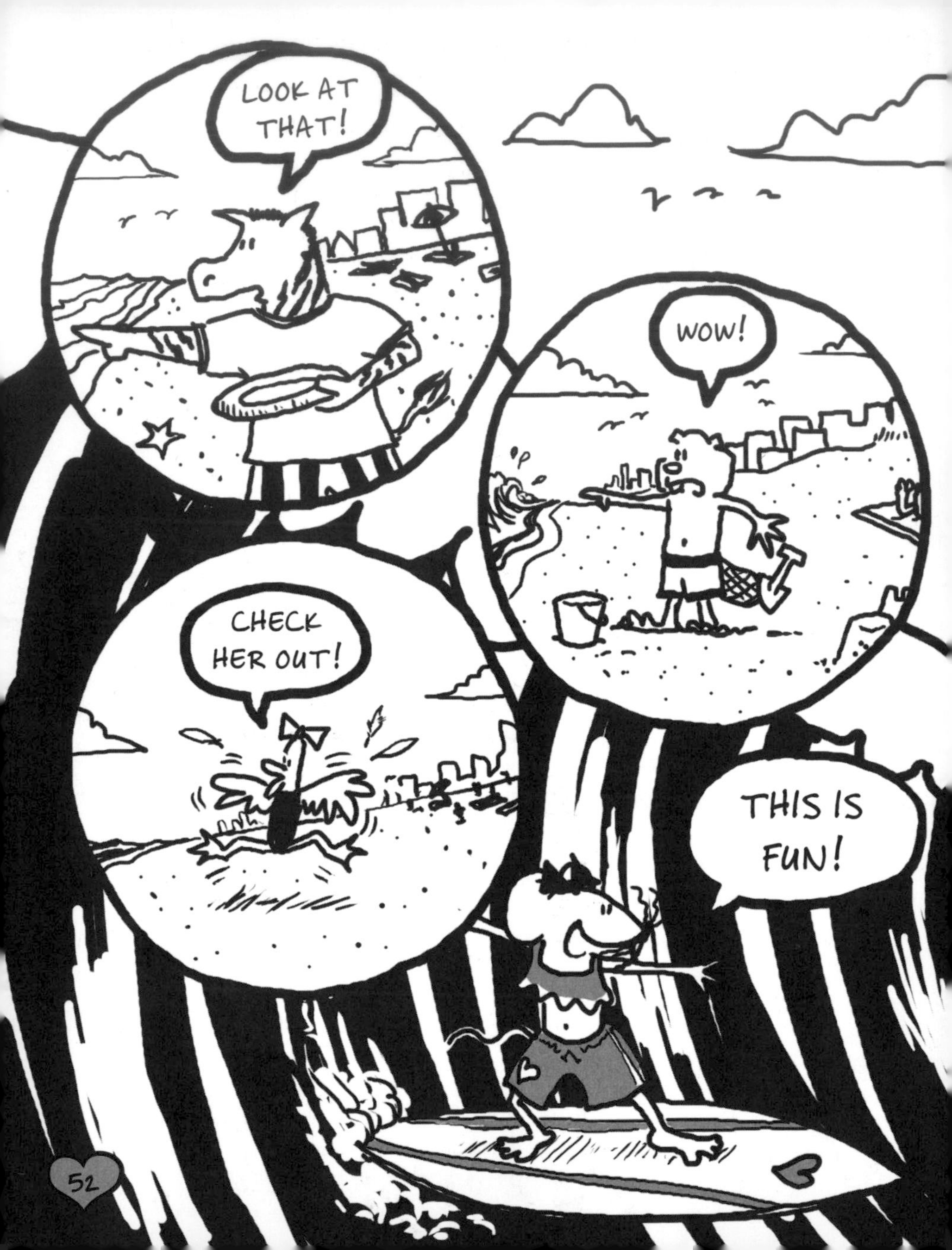
LOOK AT THAT!
WOW!
CHECK HER OUT!
THIS IS FUN!

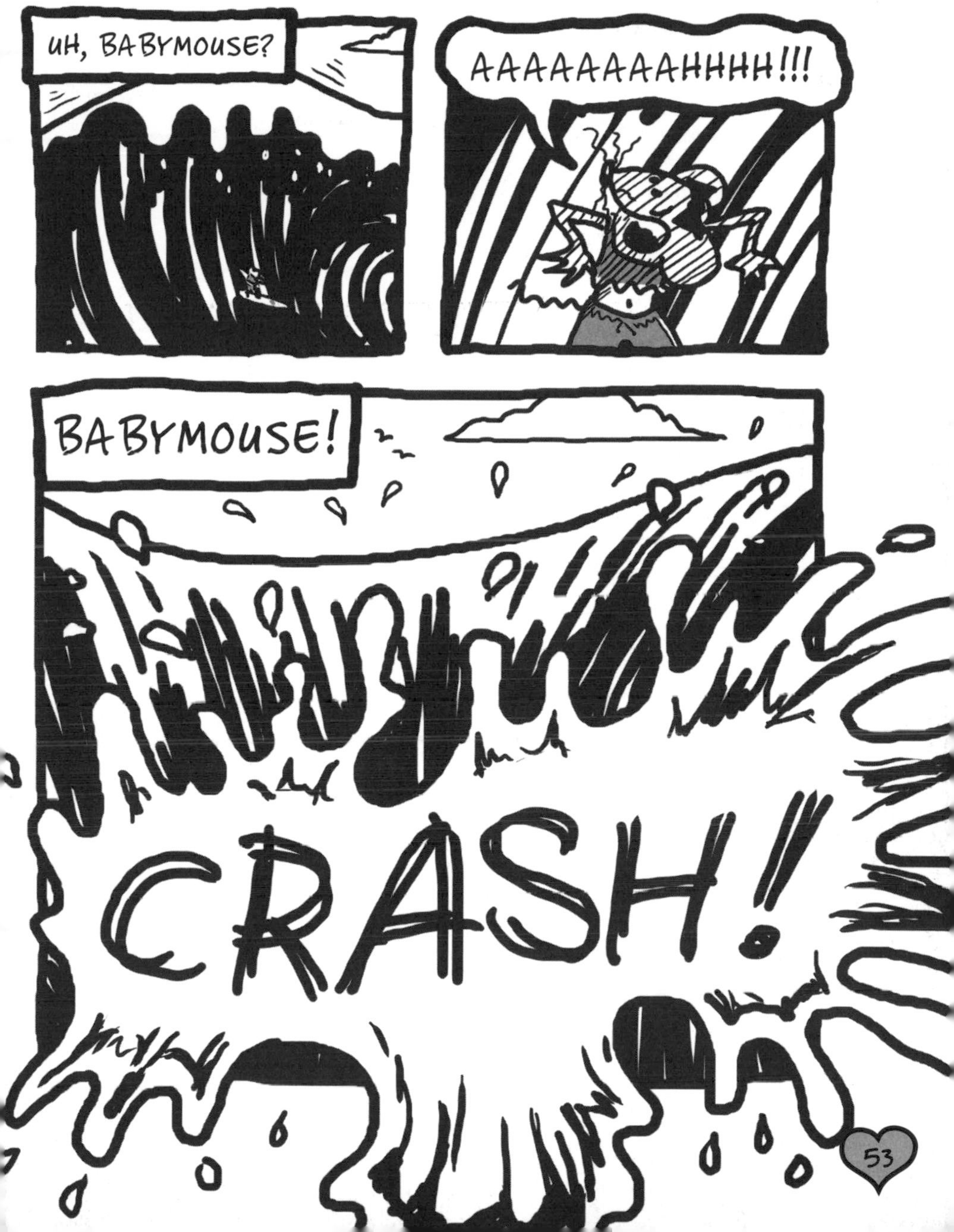
UH, BABYMOUSE?
AAAAAAAAAHHHH!!!
BABYMOUSE!
CRASH!

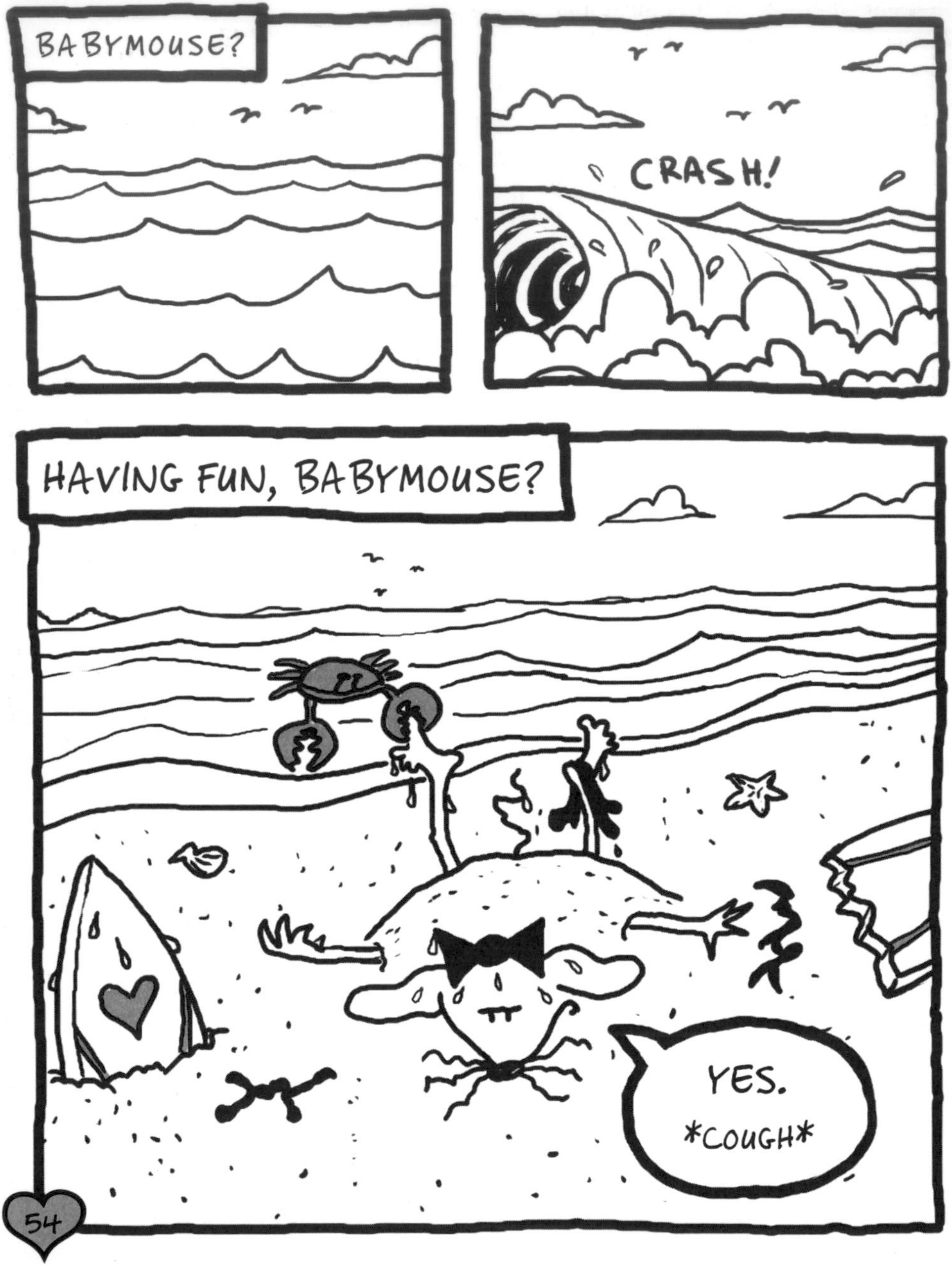
BABYMOUSE?
CRASH!
HAVING FUN, BABYMOUSE?
YES.
COUGH

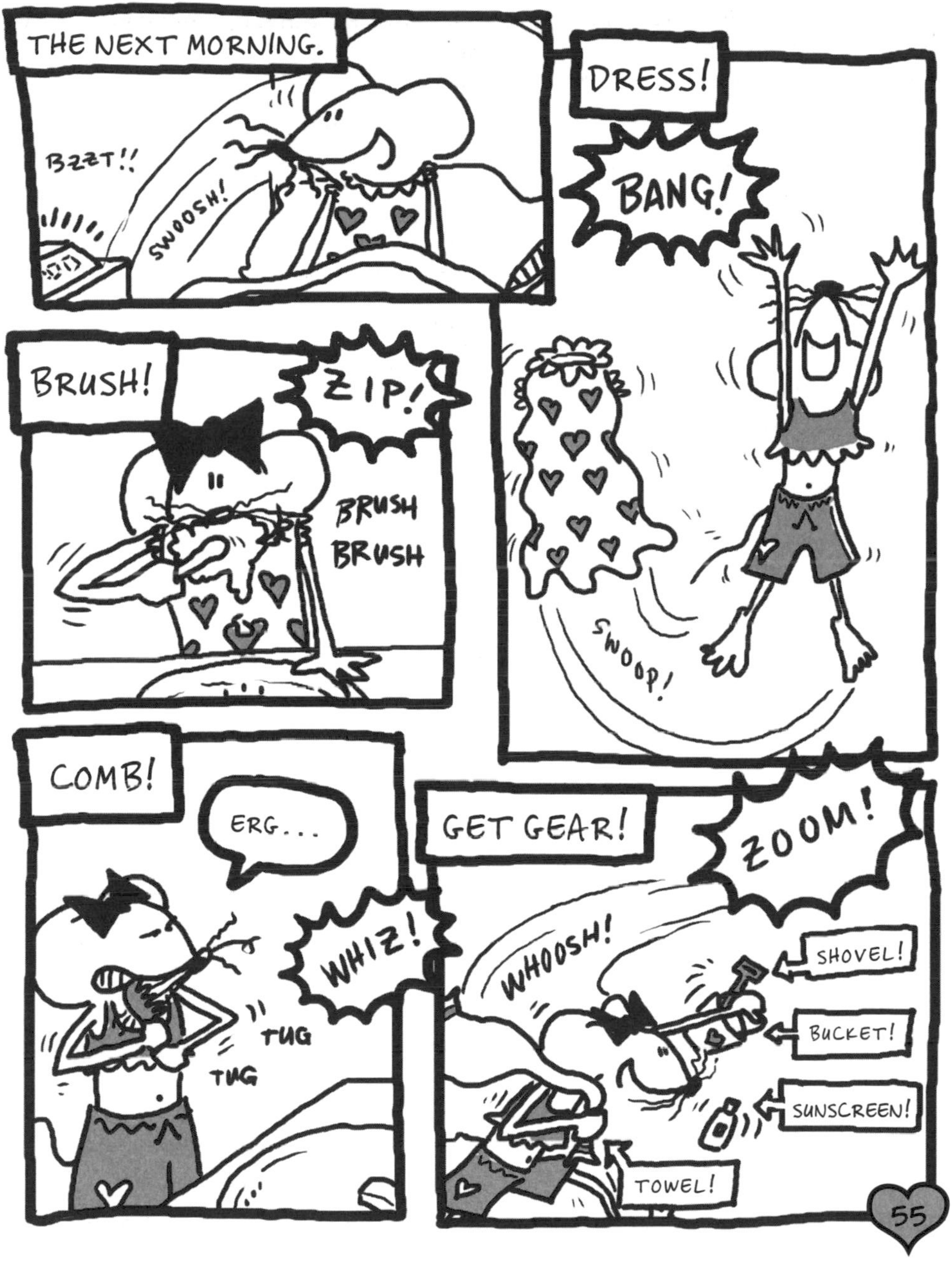

THE NEXT MORNING.
BZZT!!
SWOOSH!
BRUSH!
ZIP!
BRUSH
BRUSH
DRESS!
BANG!
SWOOP!
COMB!
ERG...
WHIZ!
TUG
TUG
GET GEAR!
ZOOM!
WHOOSH!
SHOVEL!
BUCKET!
SUNSCREEN!
TOWEL!

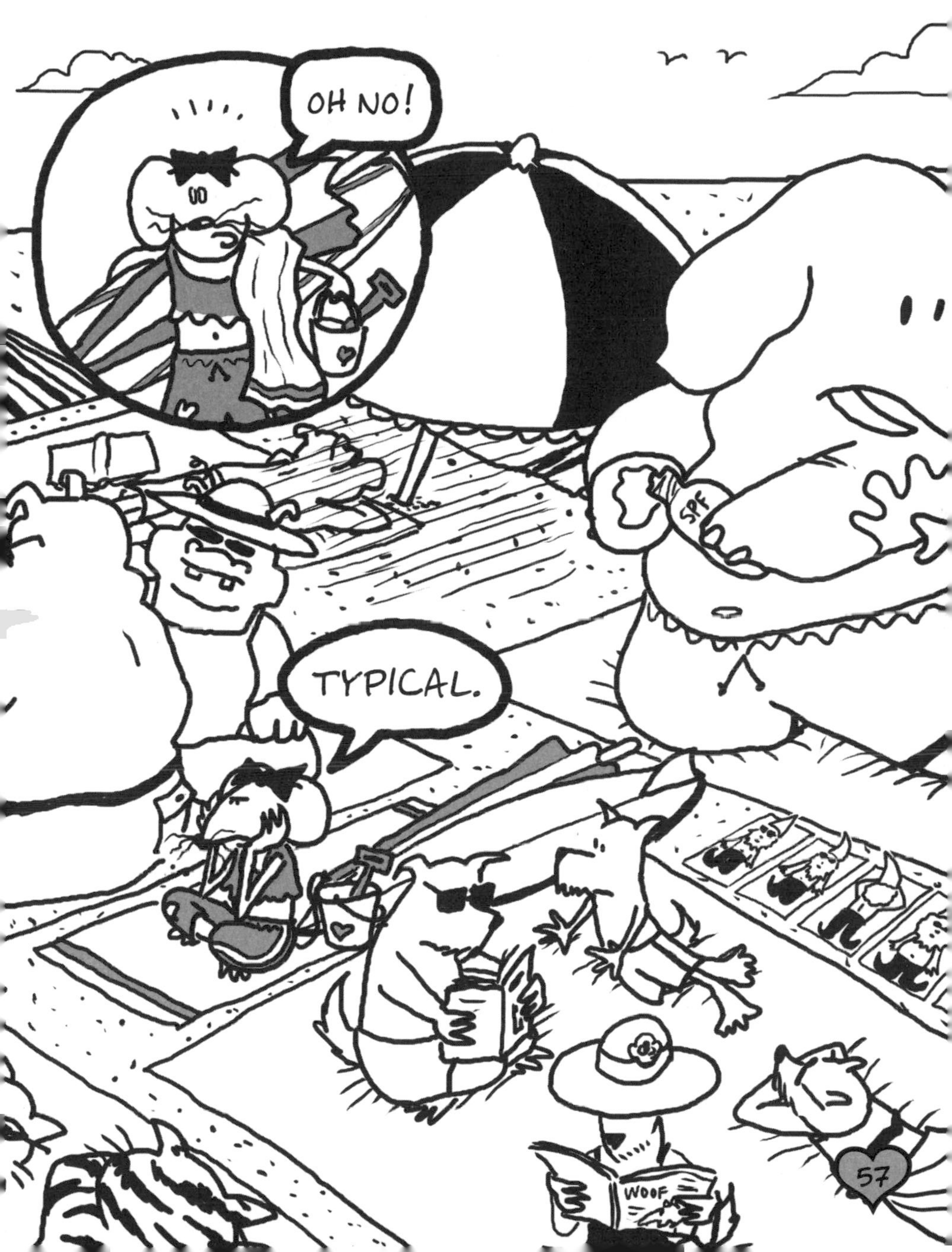
OH NO!
TYPICAL.
SPF
WOOF

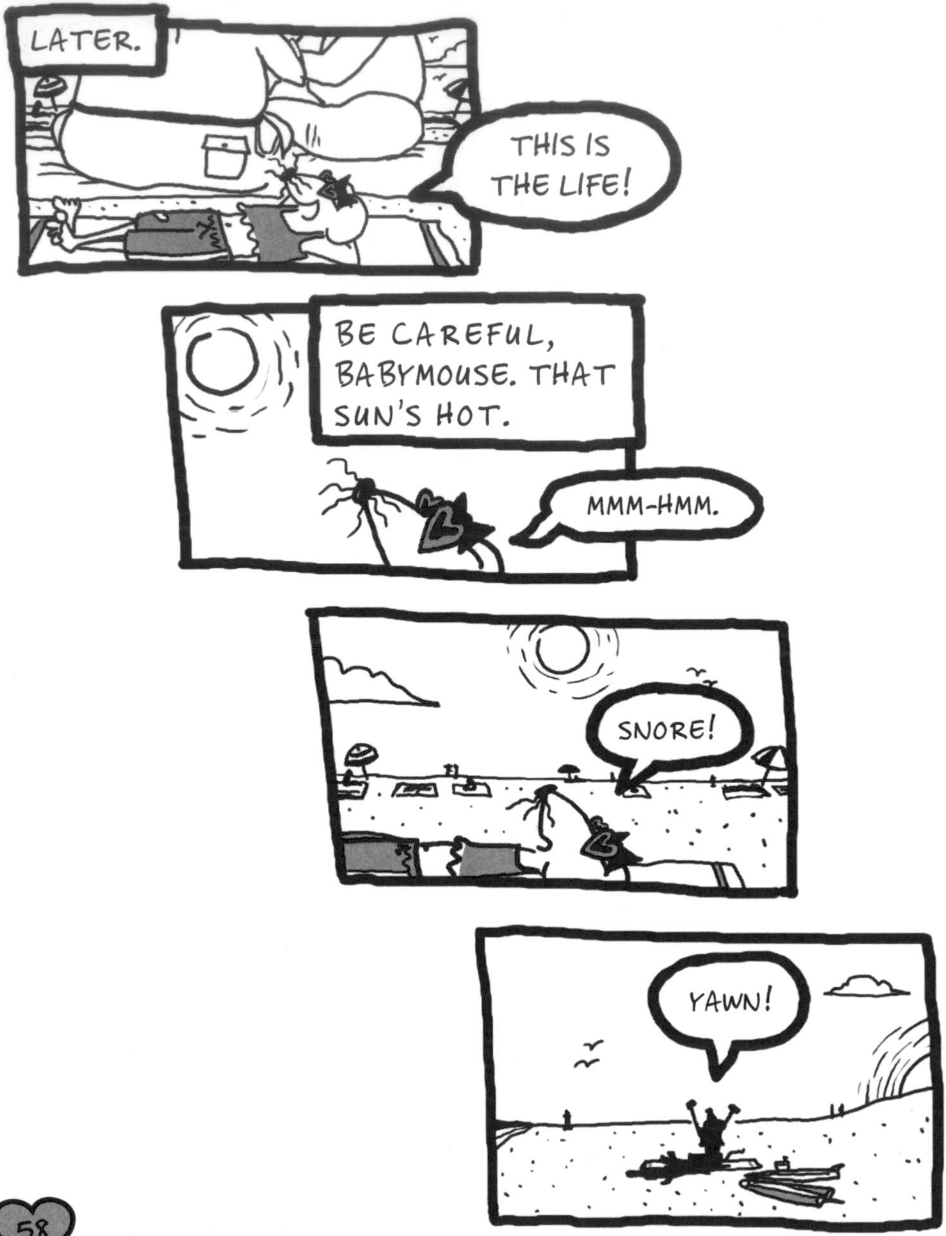
LATER.
THIS IS THE LIFE!
BE CAREFUL, BABYMOUSE. THAT SUN'S HOT.
MMM-HMM.
SNORE!
YAWN!

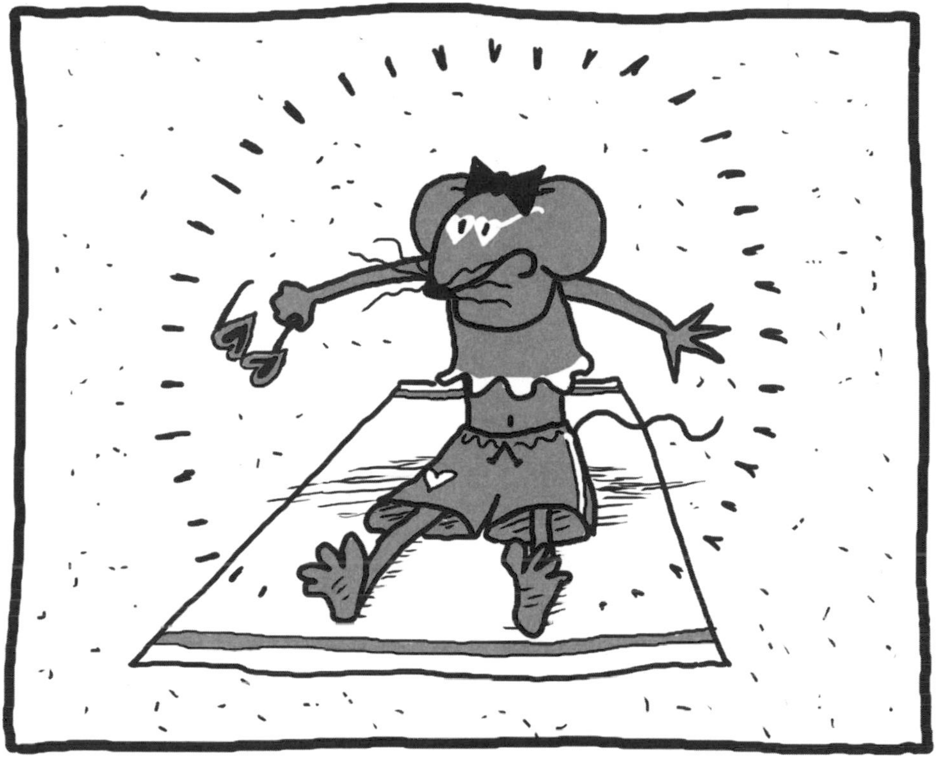

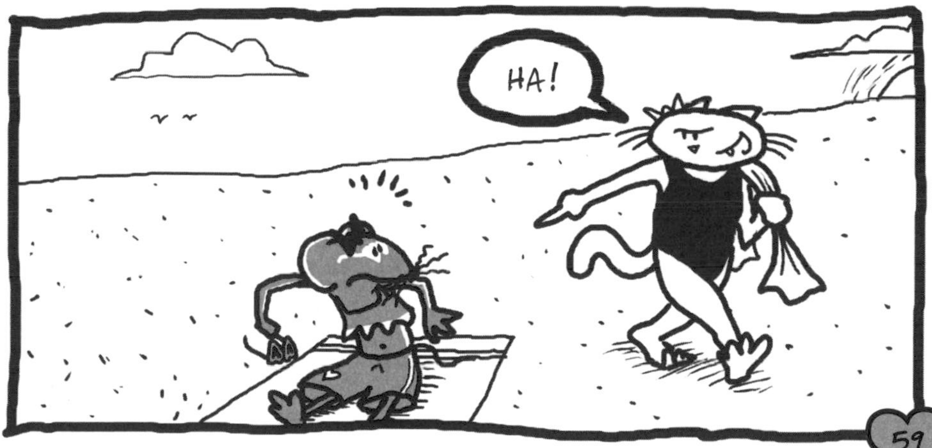
HA!

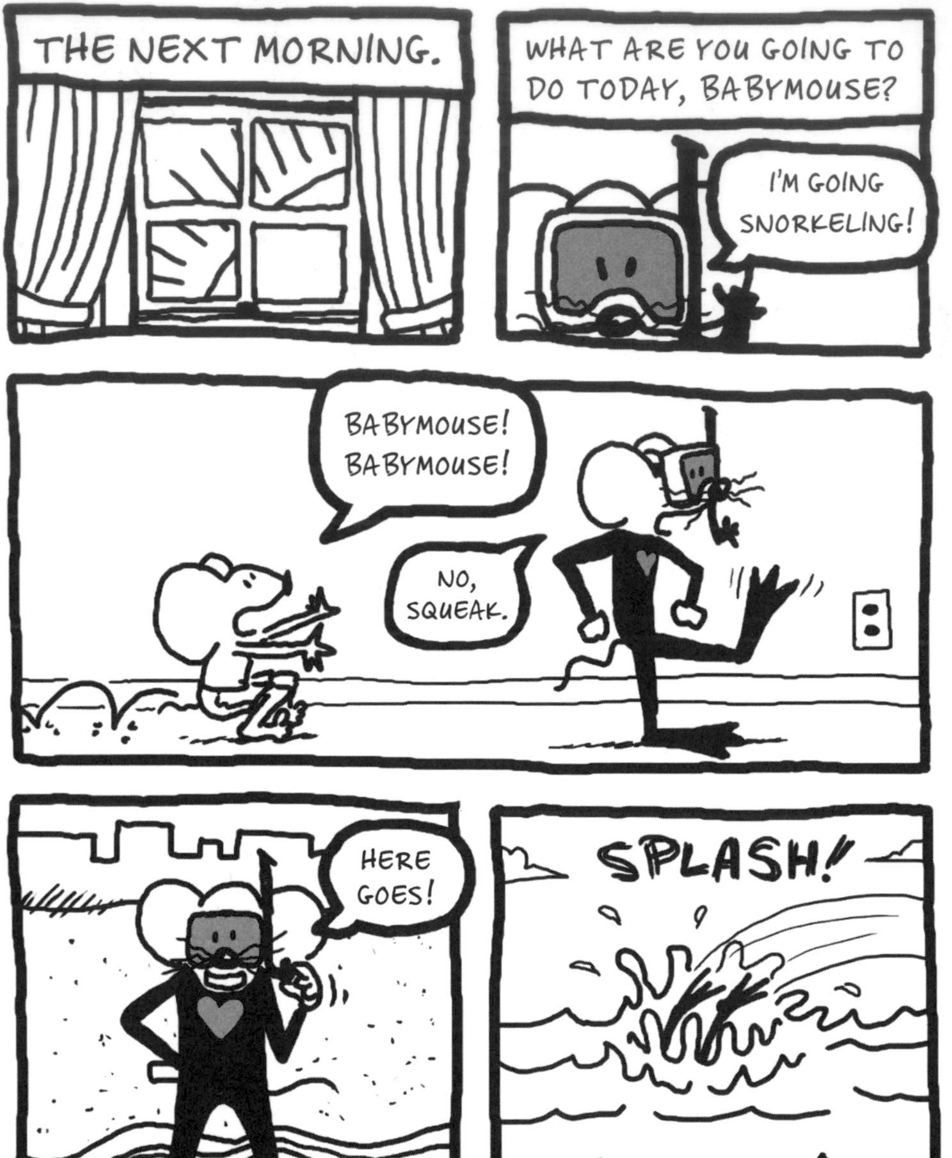
THE NEXT MORNING.
WHAT ARE YOU GOING TO DO TODAY, BABYMOUSE?
I'M GOING SNORKELING!
BABYMOUSE! BABYMOUSE!
NO, SQUEAK.
HERE GOES!
SPLASH!

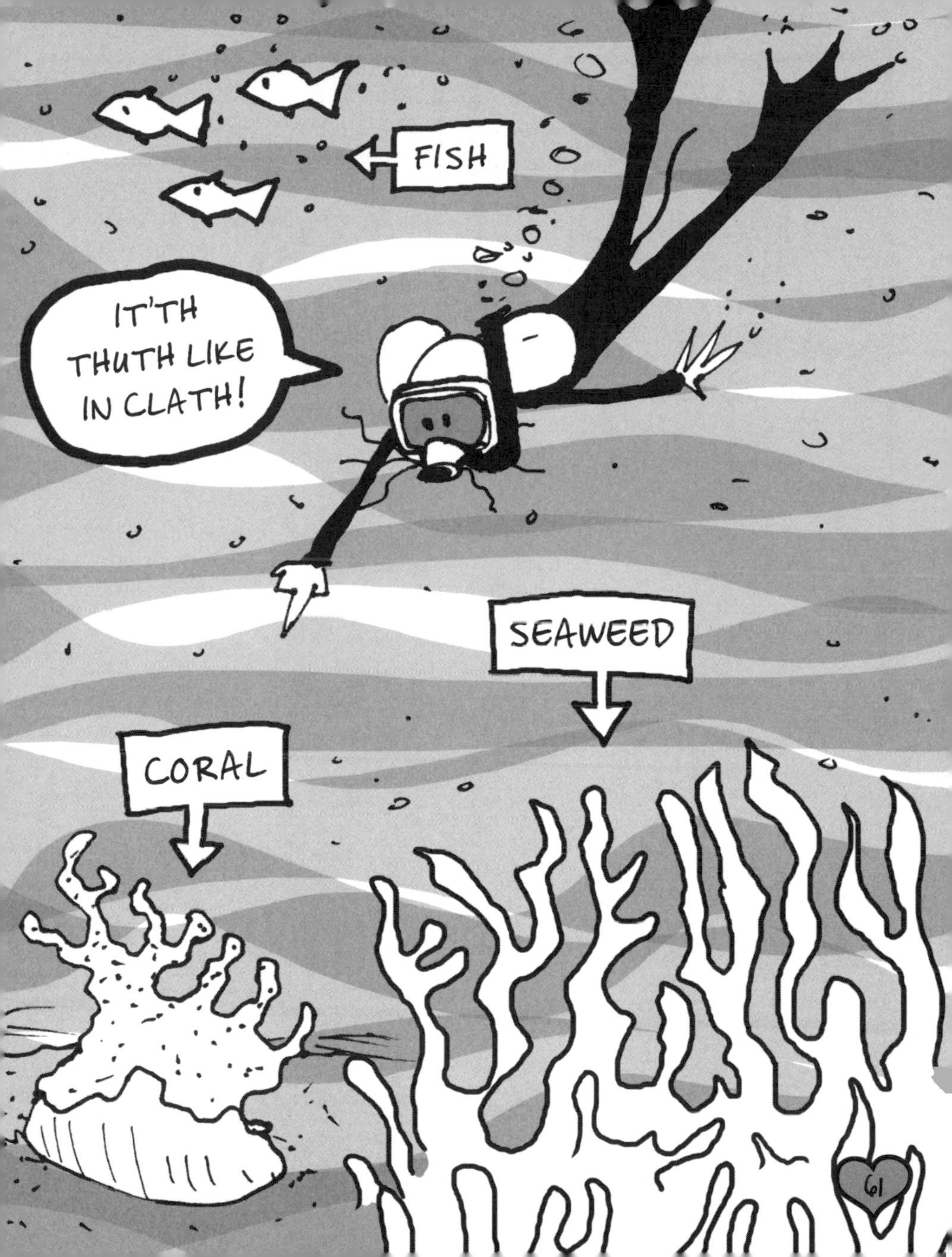
FISH
IT'TH THUTH LIKE IN CLATH!
SEAWEED
CORAL

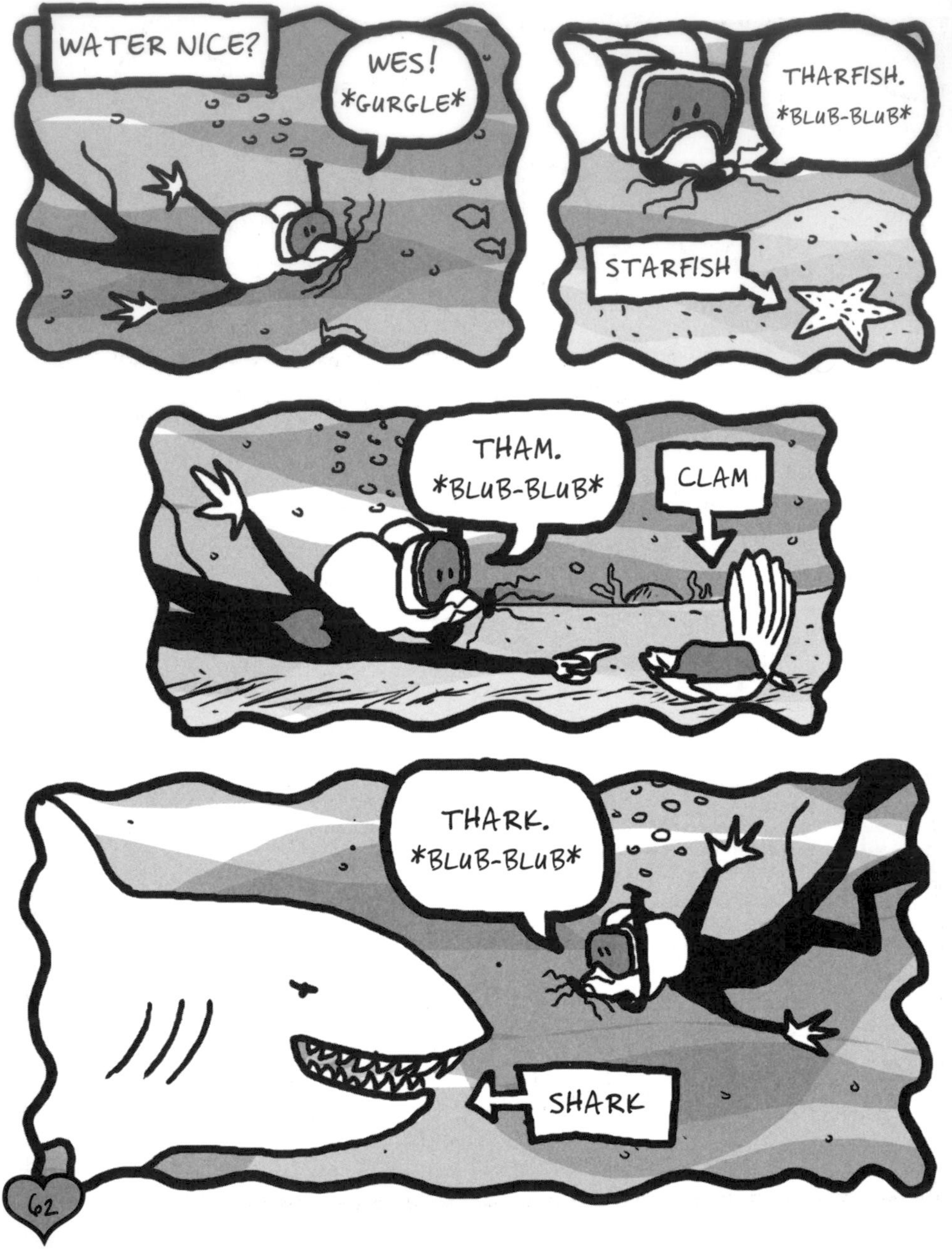
WATER NICE?
WES! *GURGLE*
THARFISH. *BLUB-BLUB*
STARFISH
THAM. *BLUB-BLUB*
CLAM
THARK. *BLUB-BLUB*
SHARK

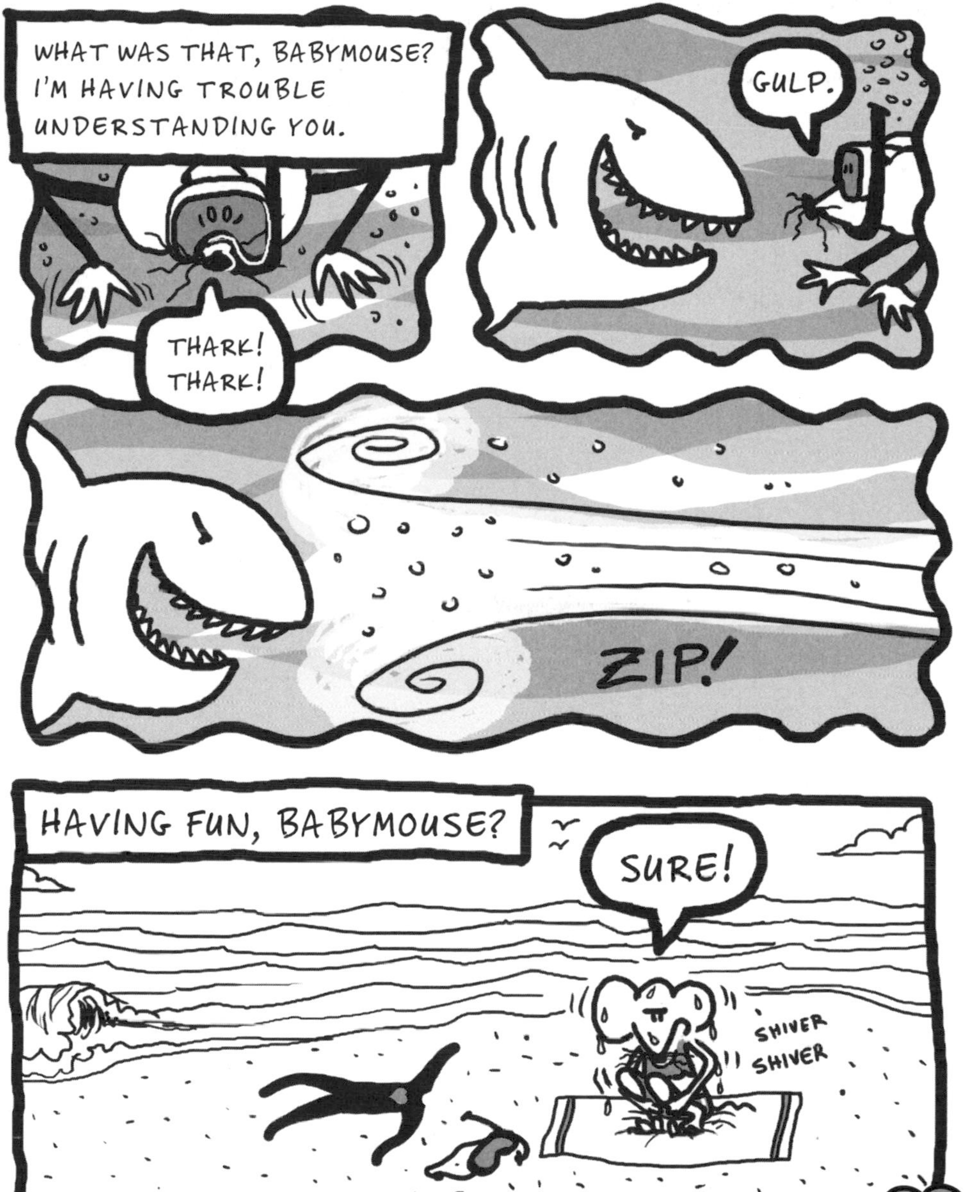

WHAT WAS THAT, BABYMOUSE? I'M HAVING TROUBLE UNDERSTANDING YOU.
THARK! THARK!
GULP.
ZIP!
HAVING FUN, BABYMOUSE?
SURE!
SHIVER SHIVER

THAT NIGHT.

WHERE ARE YOU GOING, BABYMOUSE?

THE BOARDWALK! IT'S GOING TO BE SO MUCH FUN!

FUN PARK

GAMES

WOW!

WATCH YOUR BROTHER, BABYMOUSE.

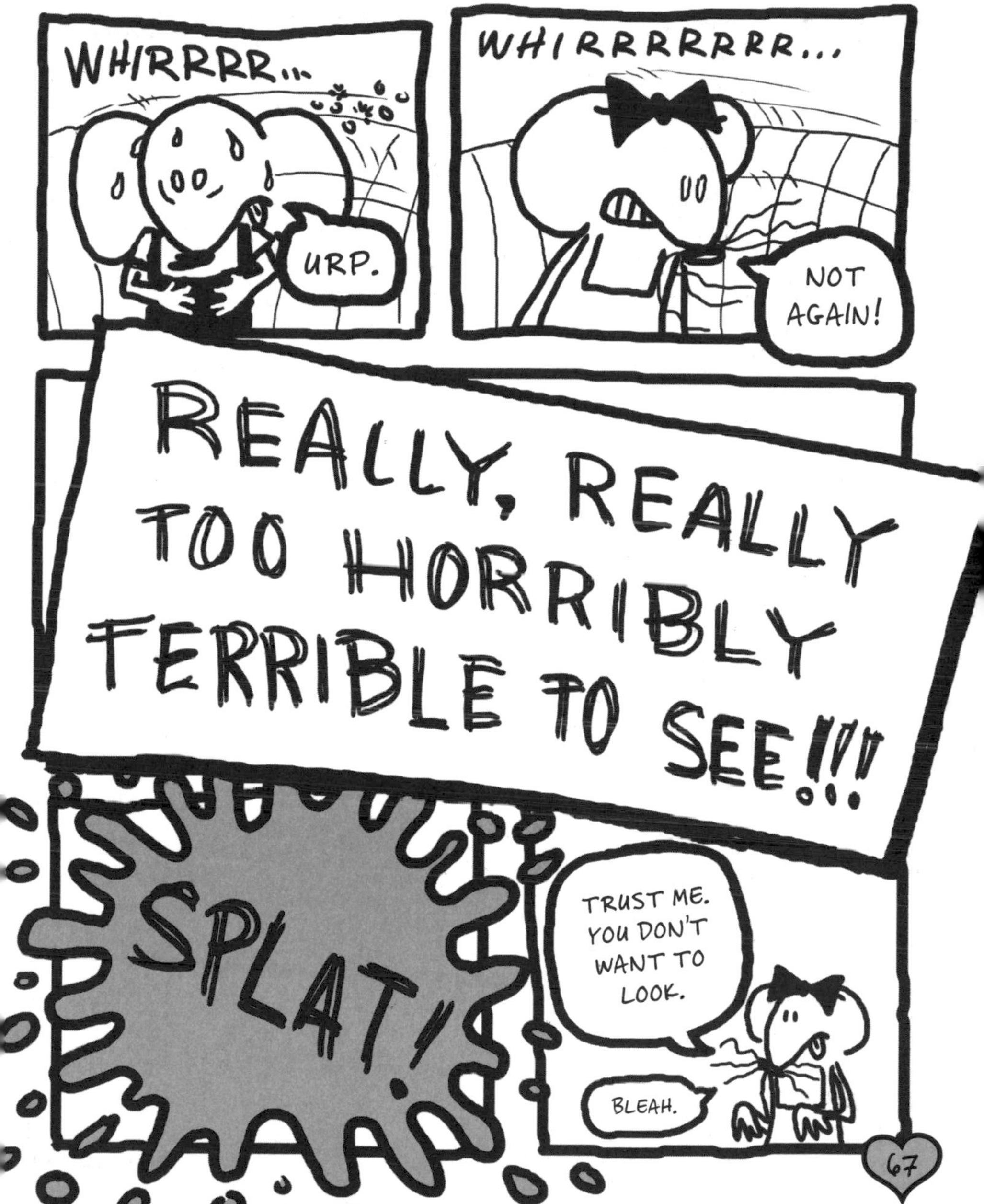
WHIRRRR...
URP.
WHIRRRRRRR...
NOT AGAIN!
REALLY, REALLY TOO HORRIBLY TERRIBLE TO SEE!!!
SPLAT!
TRUST ME. YOU DON'T WANT TO LOOK.
BLEAH.

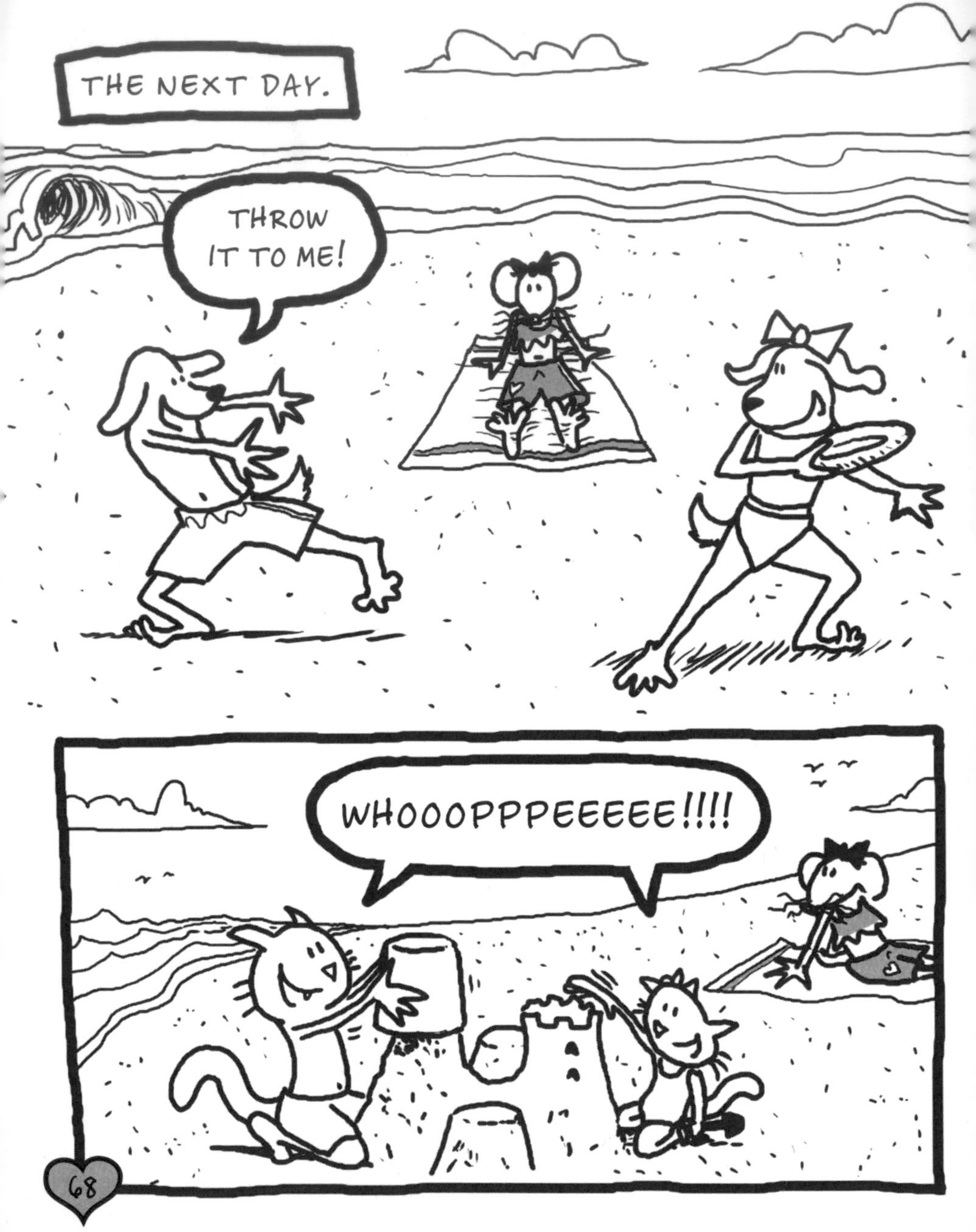
THE NEXT DAY.
THROW IT TO ME!
WHOOOPPPEEEEEE!!!!

DIG
DIG

PAT
PAT

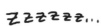

ZZZZZZZ...

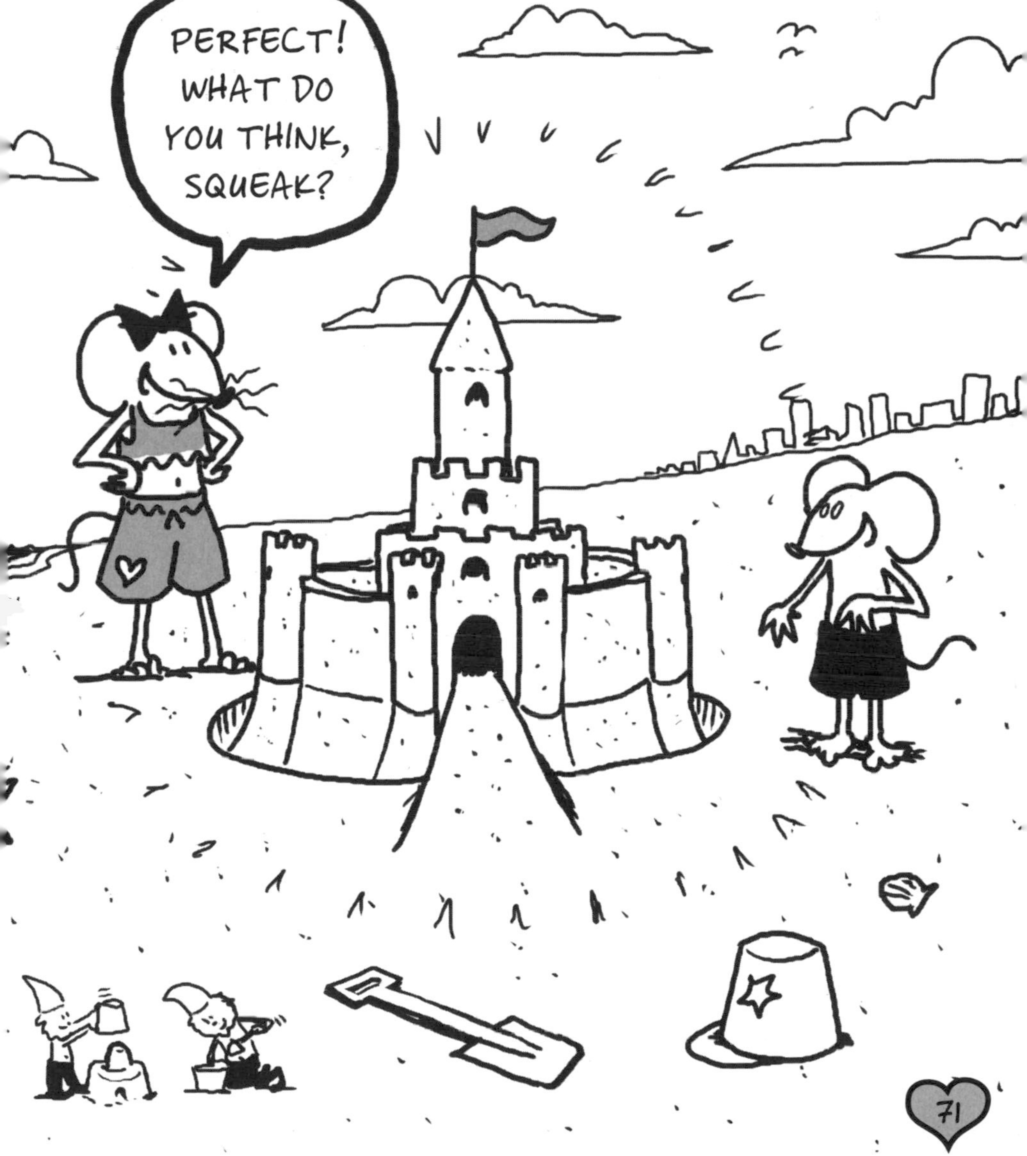
PERFECT! WHAT DO YOU THINK, SQUEAK?

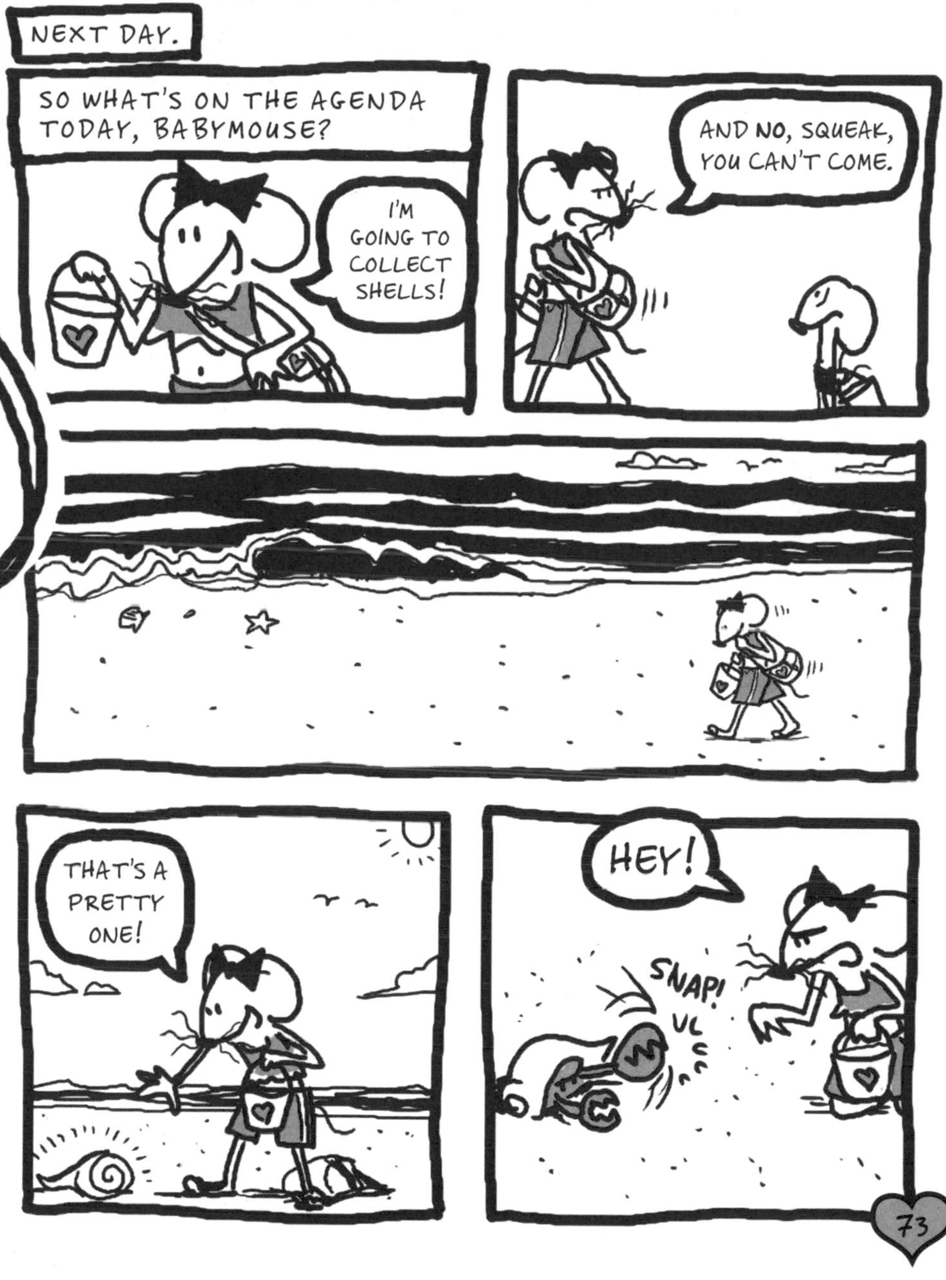
NEXT DAY.
SO WHAT'S ON THE AGENDA TODAY, BABYMOUSE?
I'M GOING TO COLLECT SHELLS!
AND NO, SQUEAK, YOU CAN'T COME.
THAT'S A PRETTY ONE!
HEY!
SNAP!

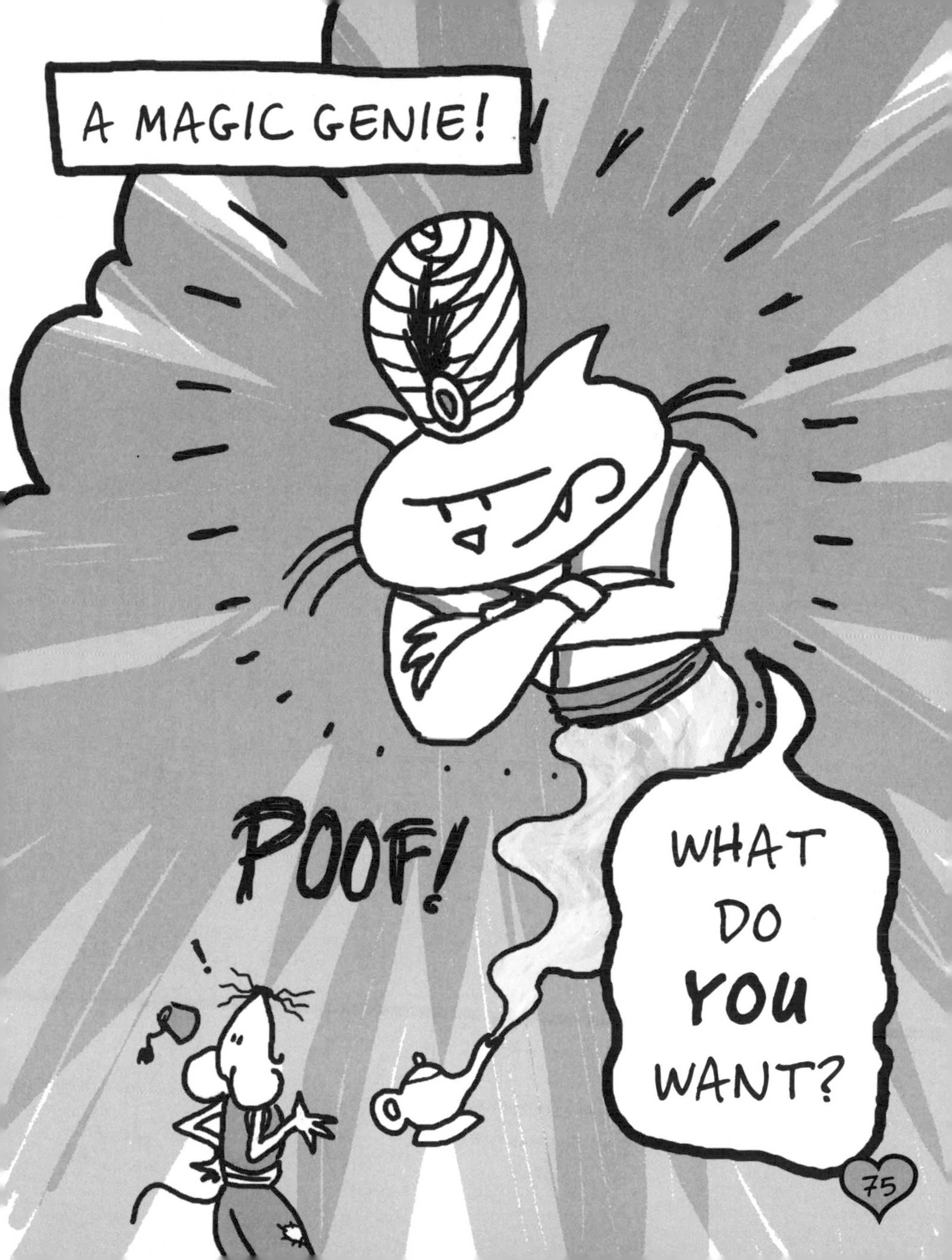
A MAGIC GENIE!
POOF!
WHAT DO YOU WANT?

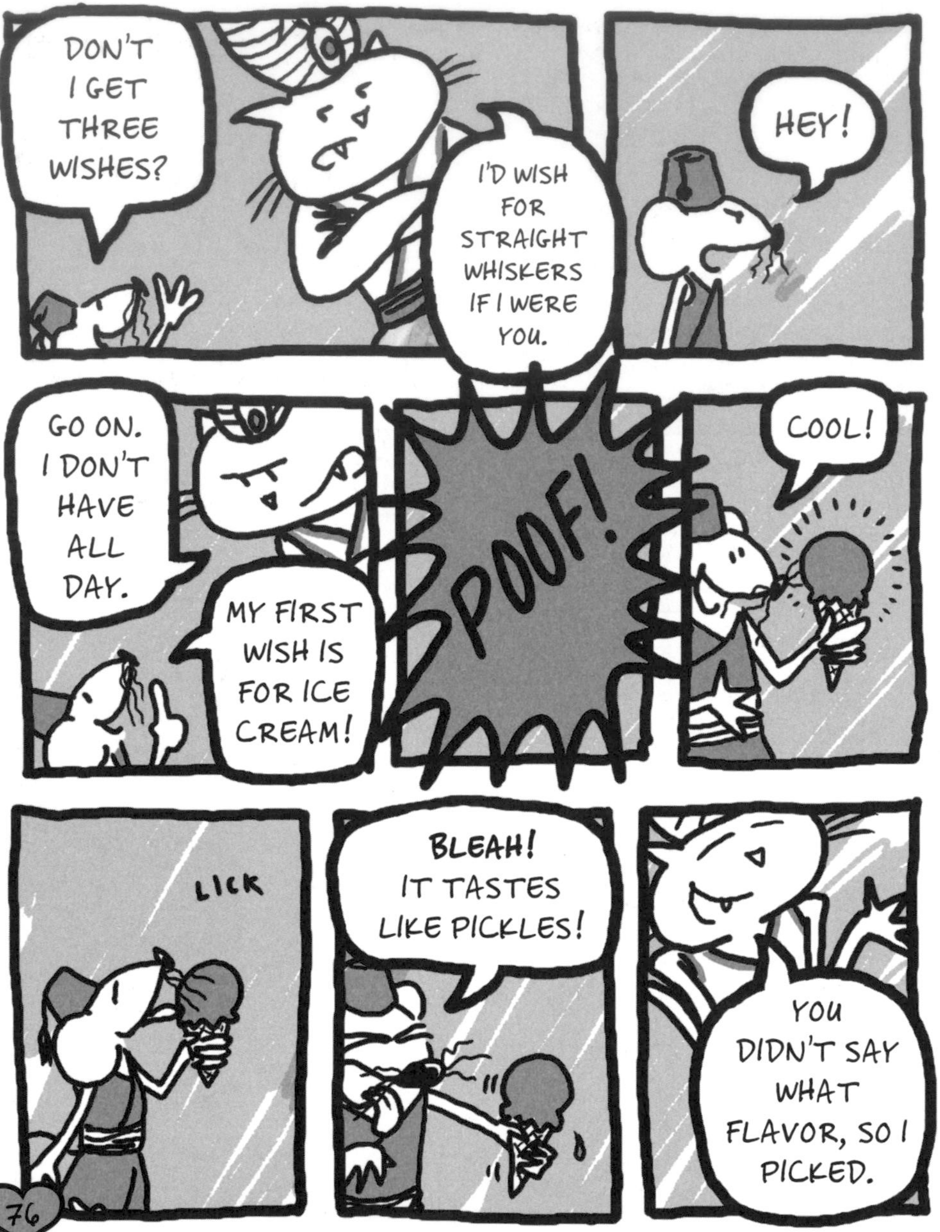
DON'T I GET THREE WISHES?
I'D WISH FOR STRAIGHT WHISKERS IF I WERE YOU.
HEY!
GO ON. I DON'T HAVE ALL DAY.
MY FIRST WISH IS FOR ICE CREAM!
SPOOF!
COOL!
LICK
BLEAH! IT TASTES LIKE PICKLES!
YOU DIDN'T SAY WHAT FLAVOR, SO I PICKED.

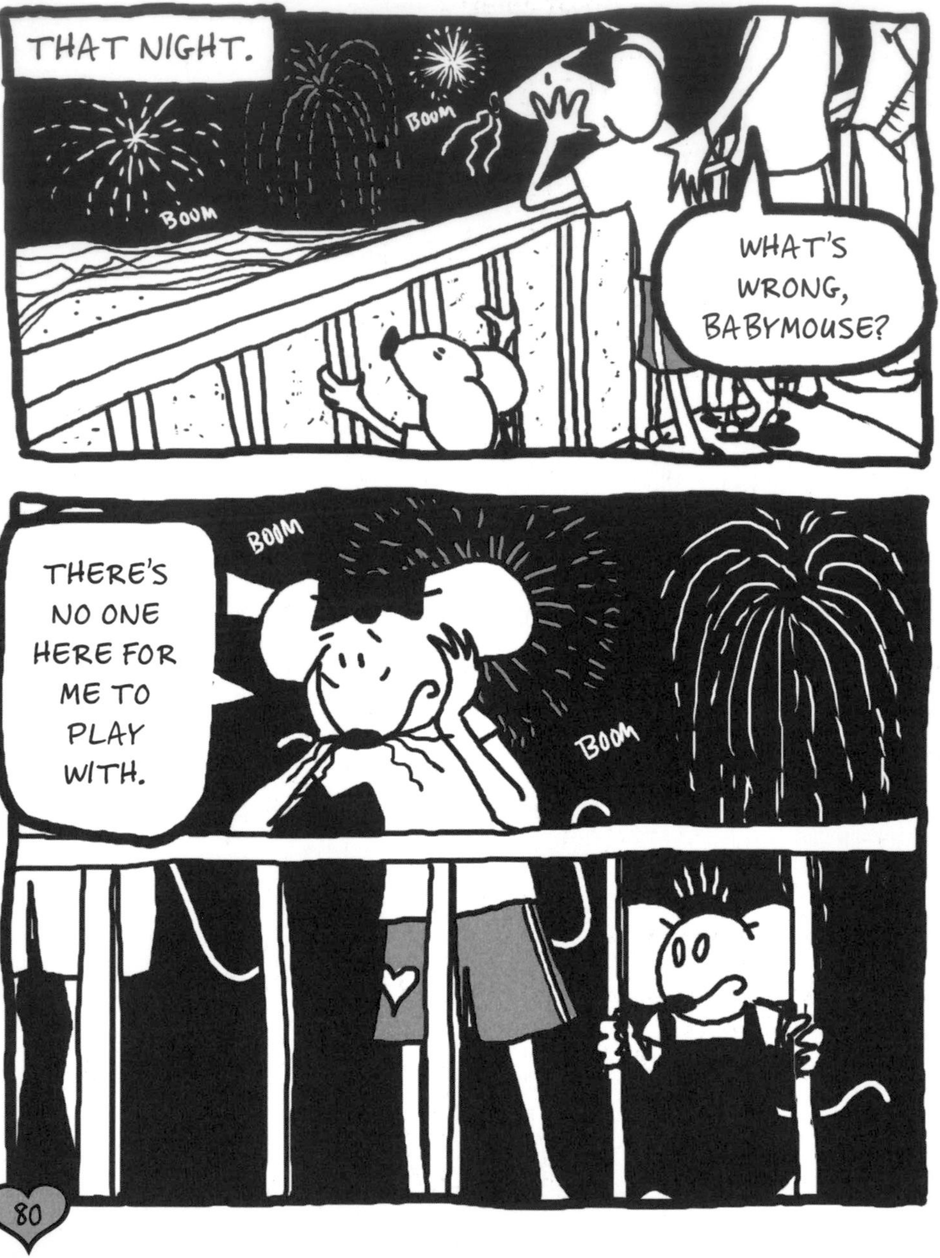
THAT NIGHT.
BOOM
BOOM
WHAT'S WRONG, BABYMOUSE?
BOOM
THERE'S NO ONE HERE FOR ME TO PLAY WITH.
BOOM

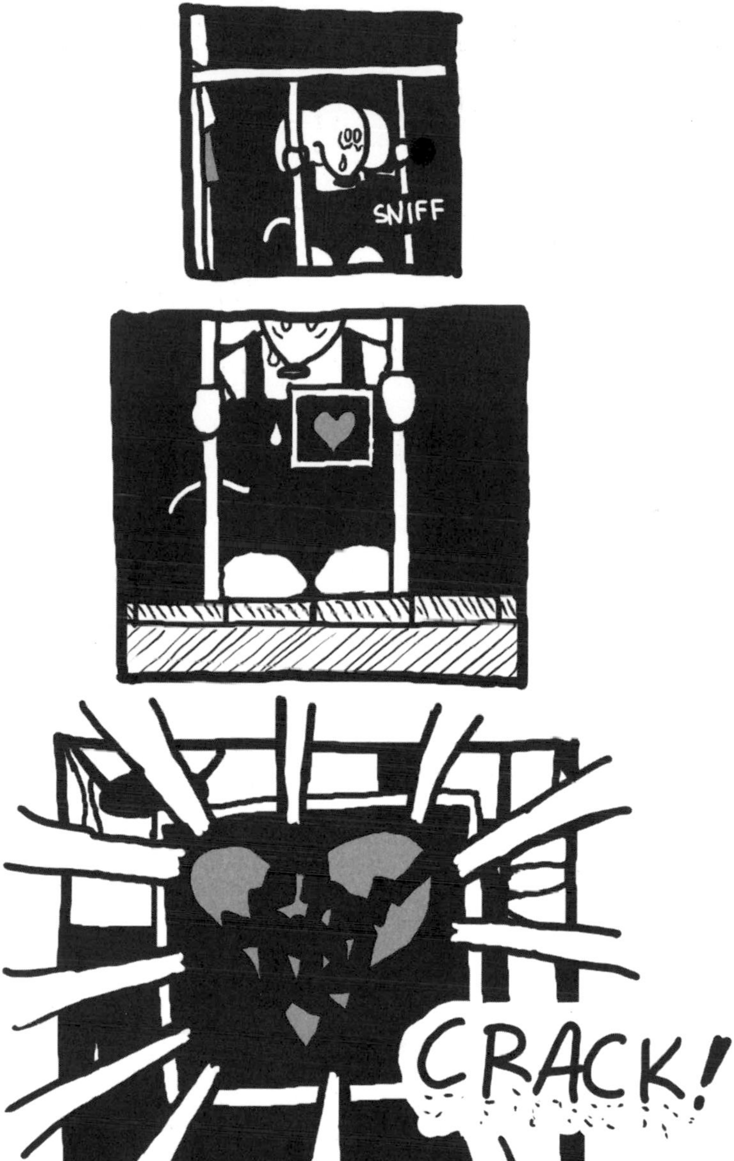
SNIFF
CRACK!

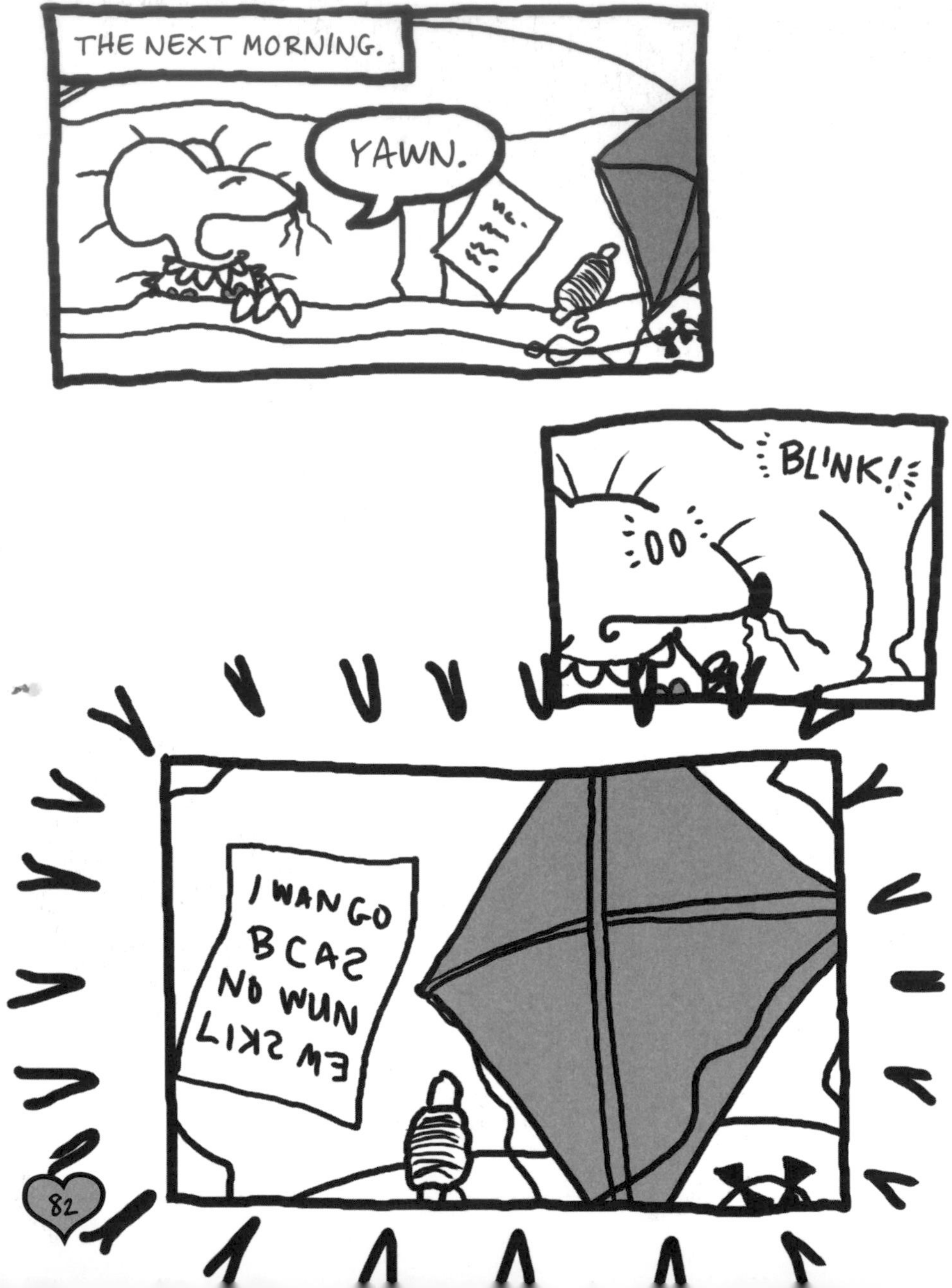
THE NEXT MORNING.
YAWN.
BLINK!
I WANGO
BCAS
NO WUN
LIKS ME

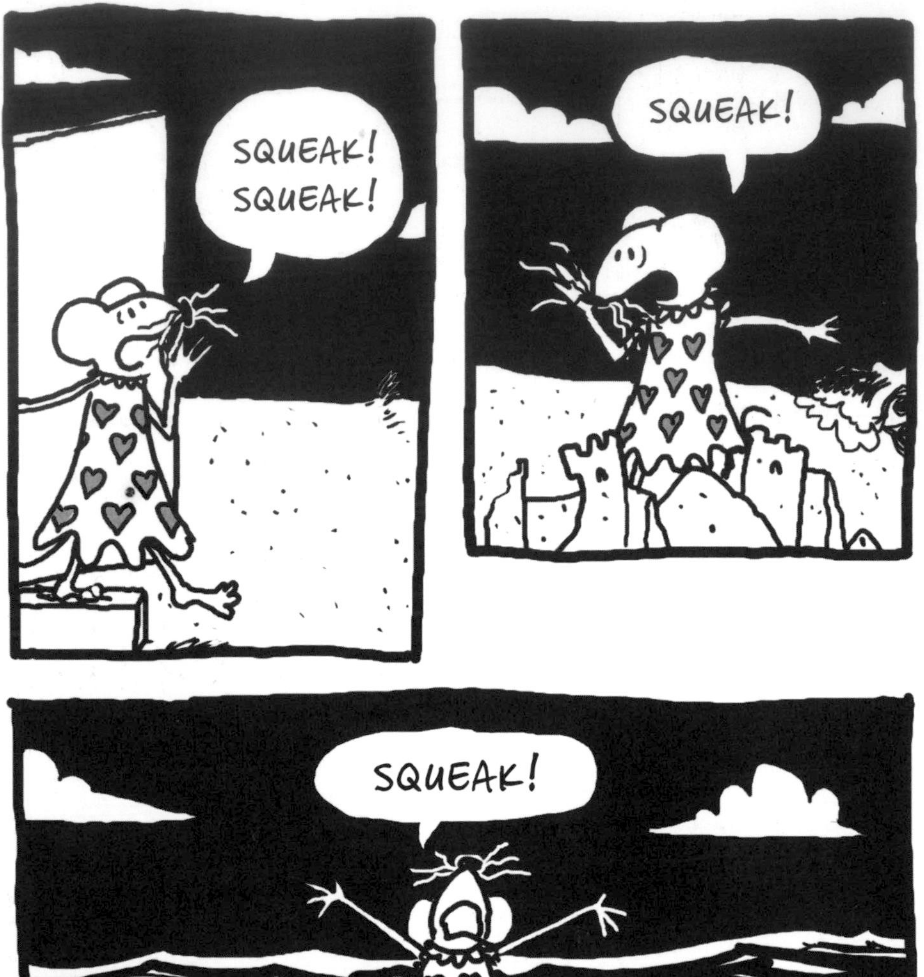
SQUEAK! SQUEAK!
SQUEAK!
SQUEAK!

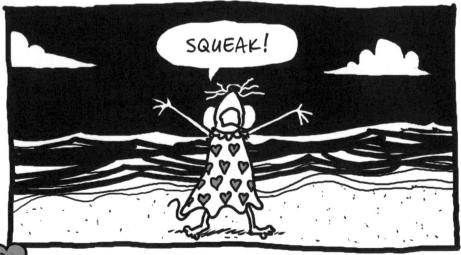

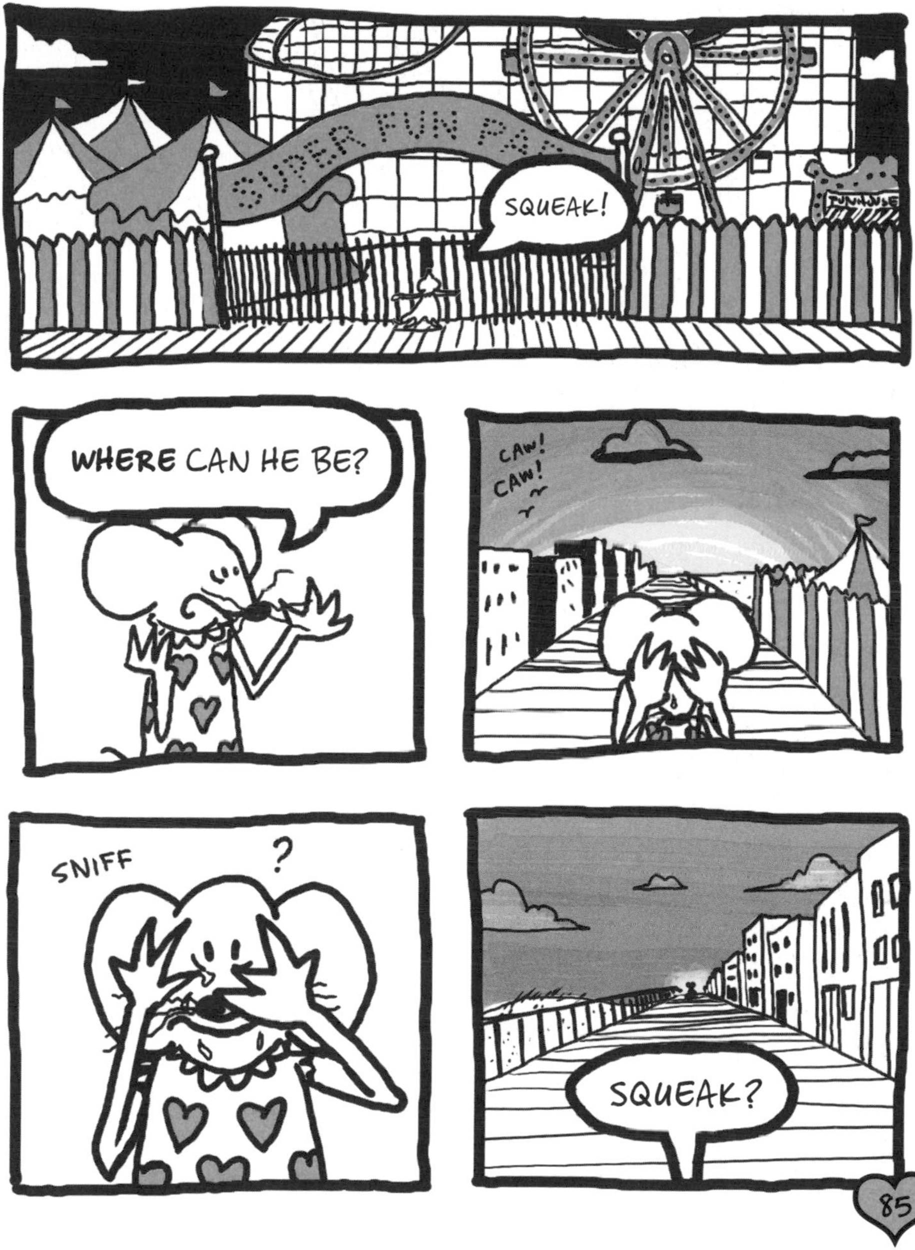
SUPER FUN PA
FUNHOUSE
SQUEAK!
WHERE CAN HE BE?
CAW!
CAW!
SNIFF
?
SQUEAK?

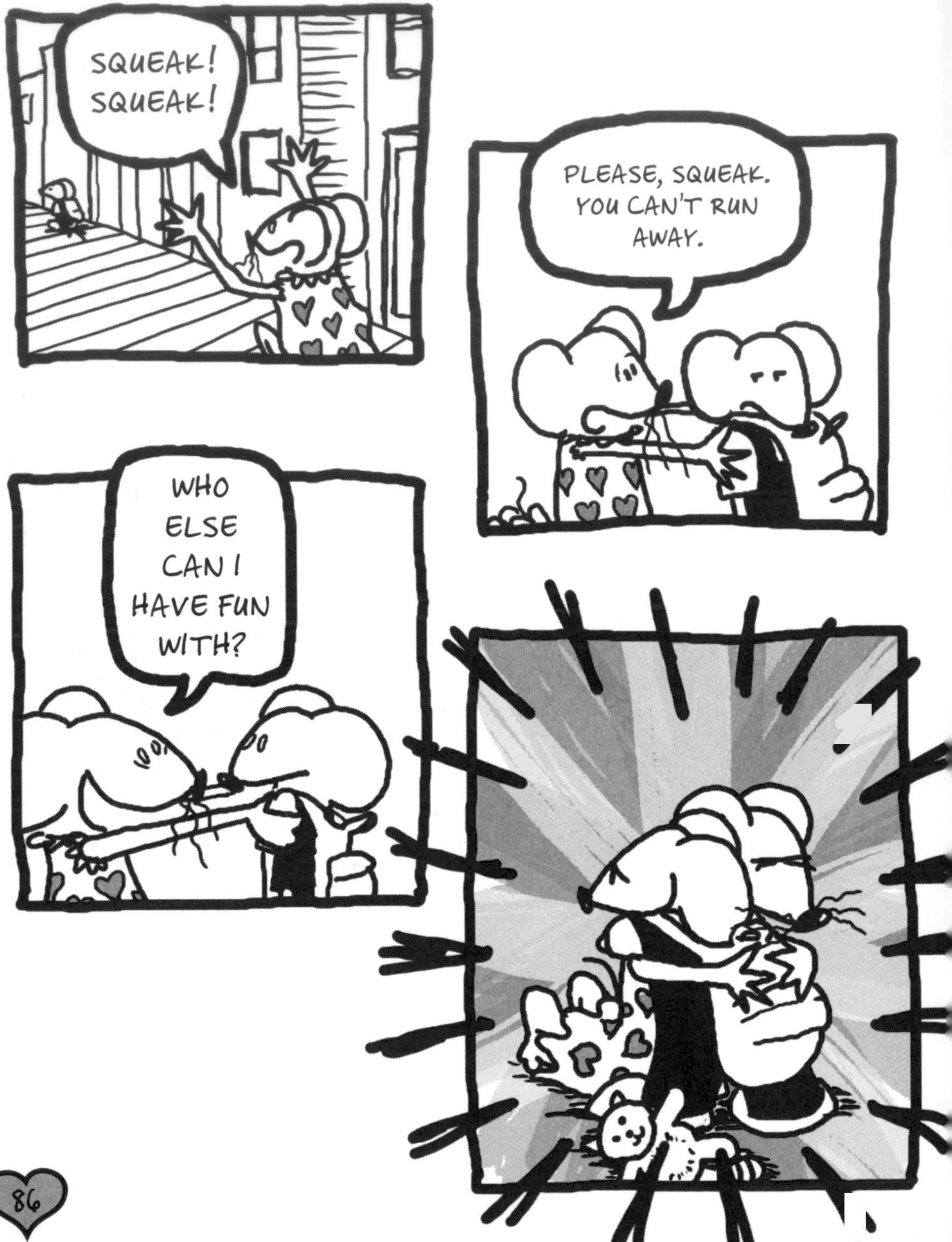
SQUEAK! SQUEAK!
PLEASE, SQUEAK. YOU CAN'T RUN AWAY.
WHO ELSE CAN I HAVE FUN WITH?

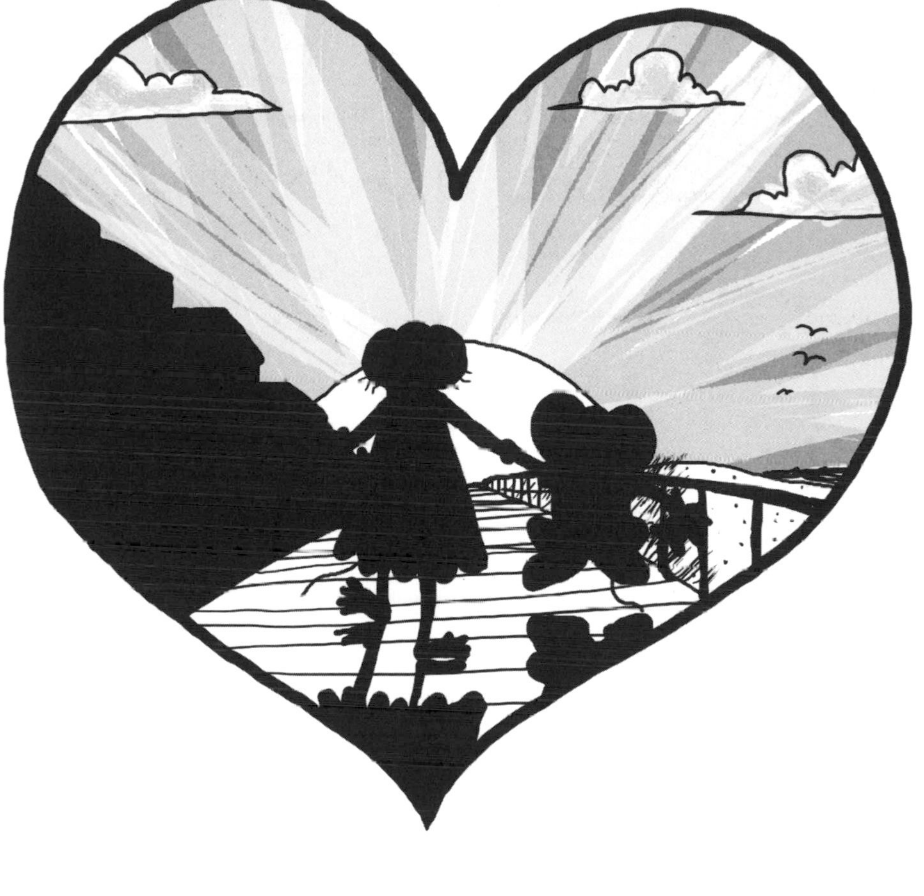

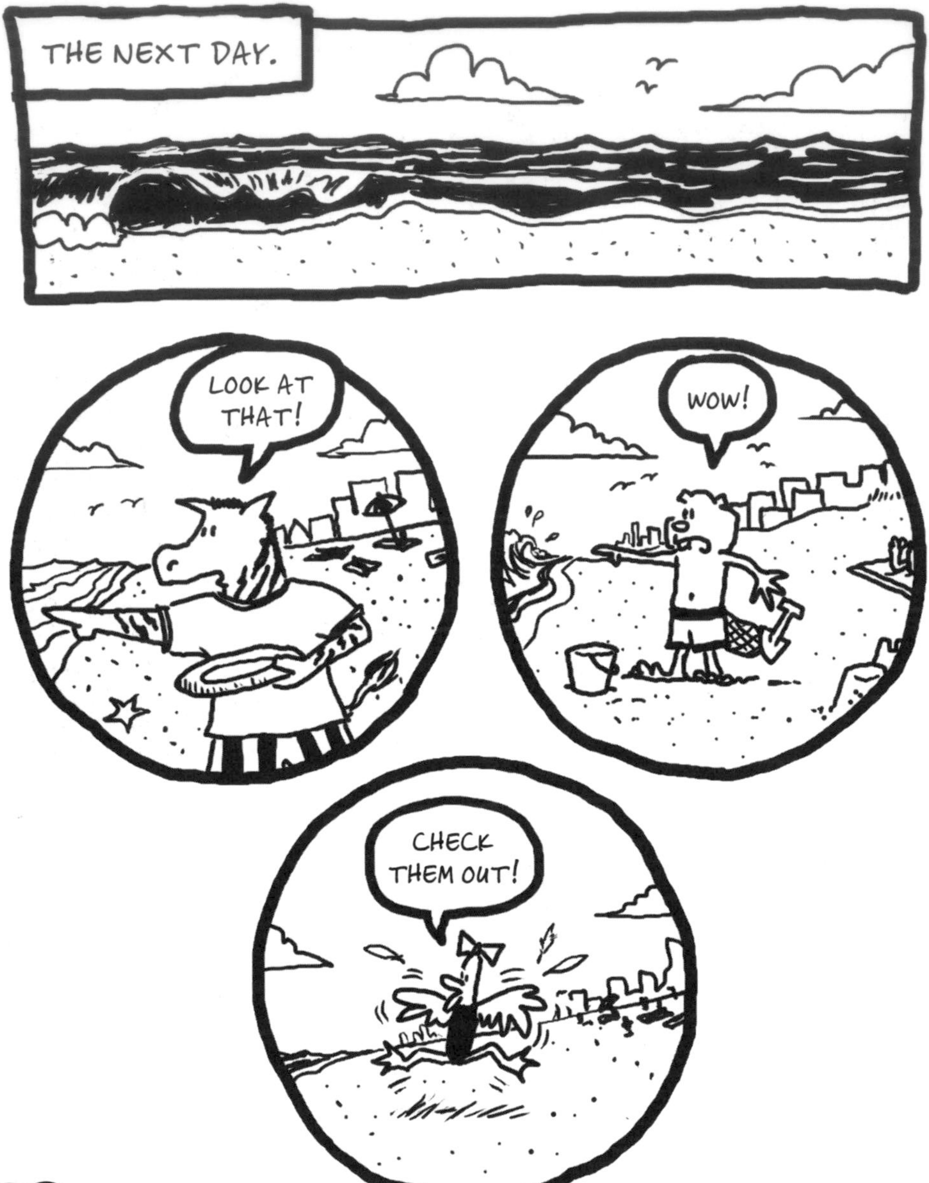
THE NEXT DAY.
LOOK AT THAT!
WOW!
CHECK THEM OUT!

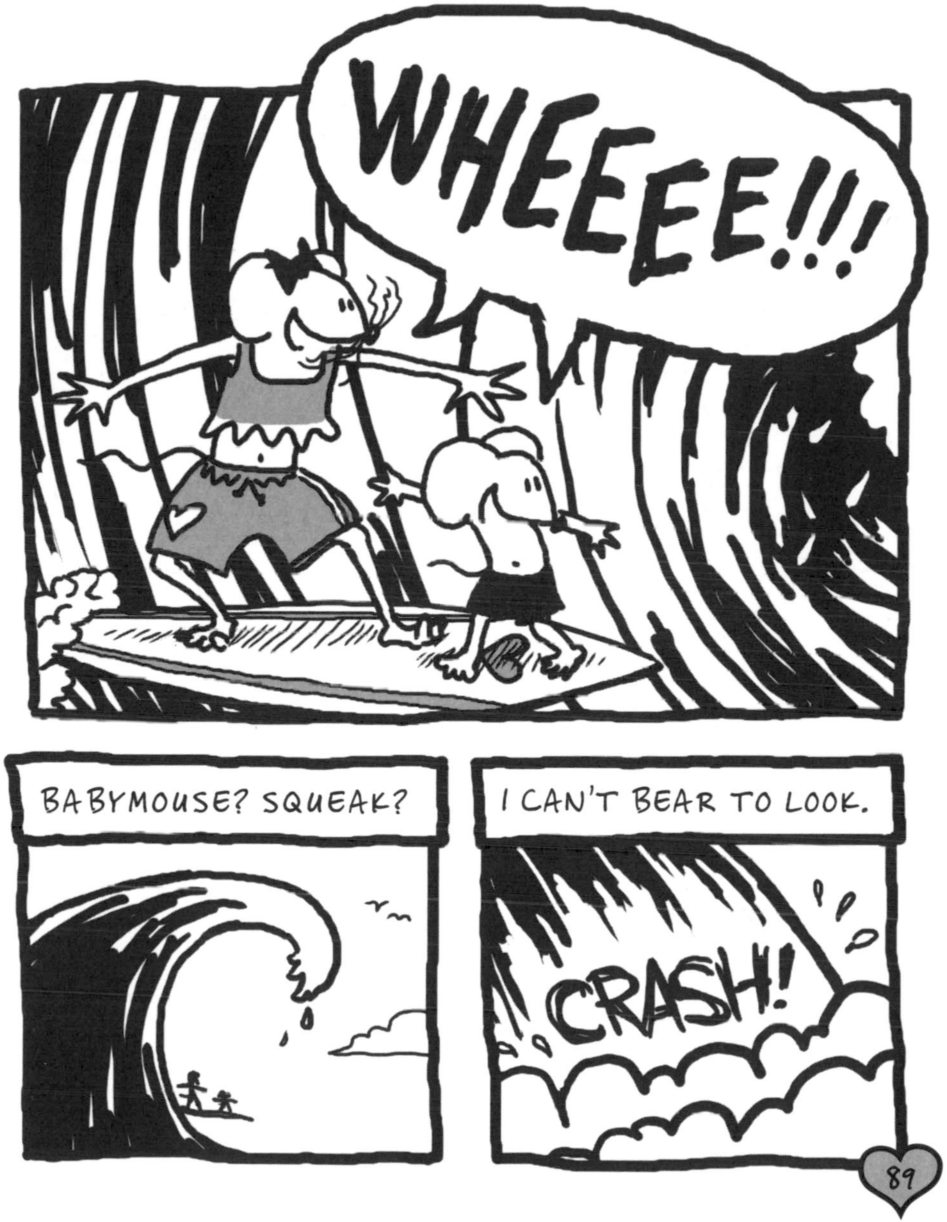
WHEEEEE!!!
BABYMOUSE? SQUEAK?
I CAN'T BEAR TO LOOK.
CRASH!

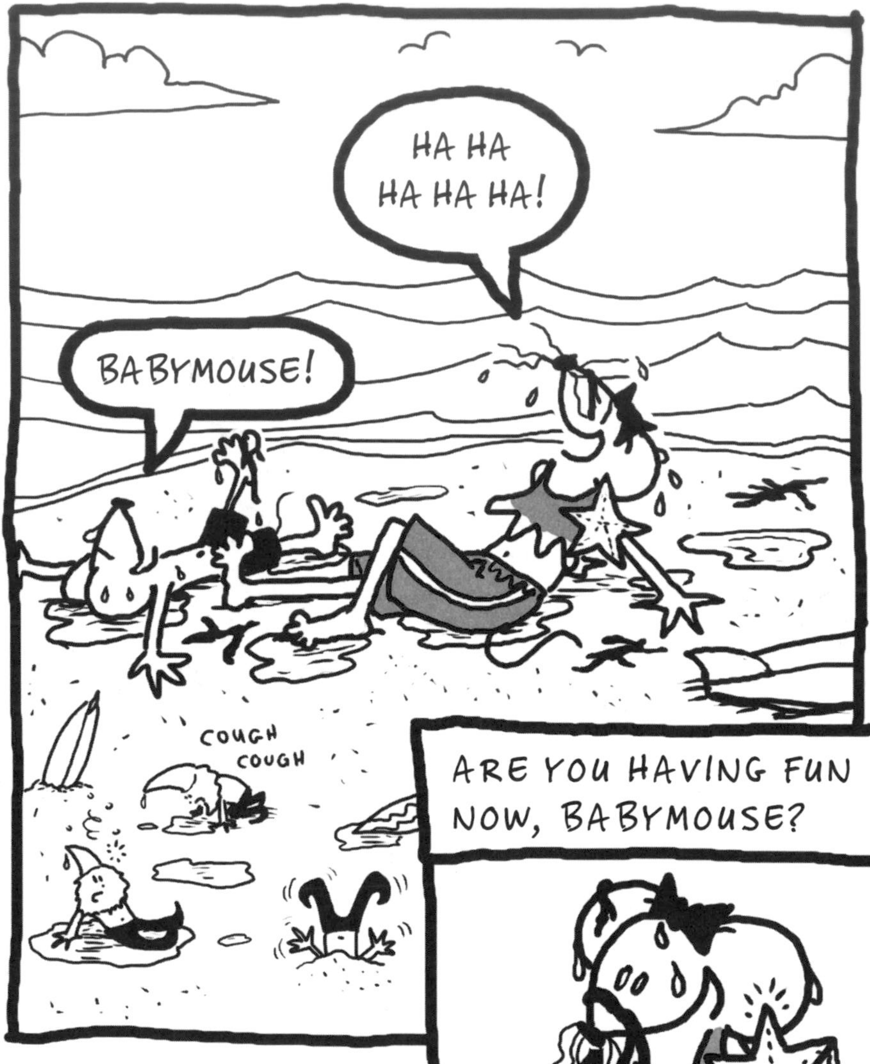
BABYMOUSE!
HA HA
HA HA HA!
COUGH
COUGH
ARE YOU HAVING FUN
NOW, BABYMOUSE?

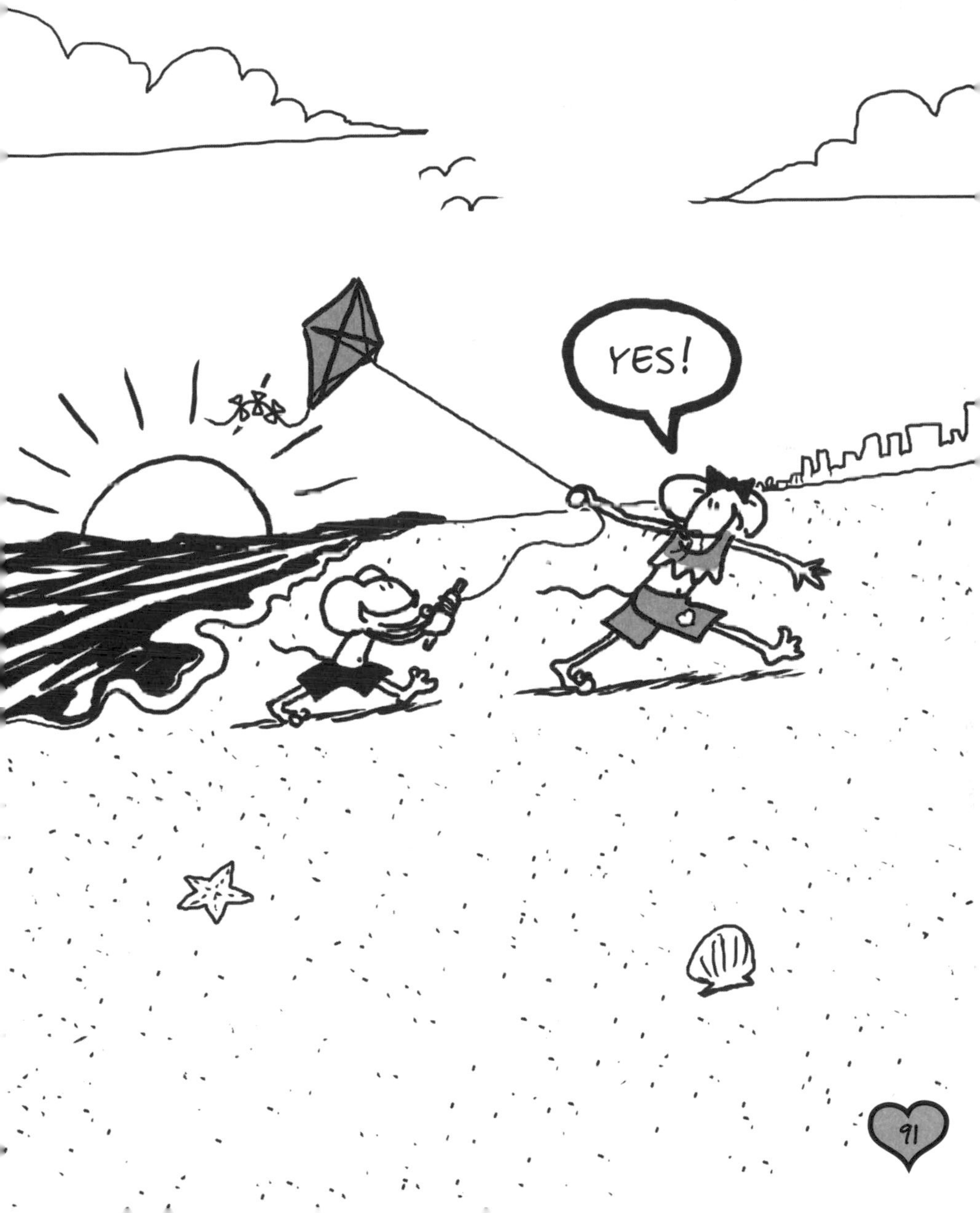
YES!

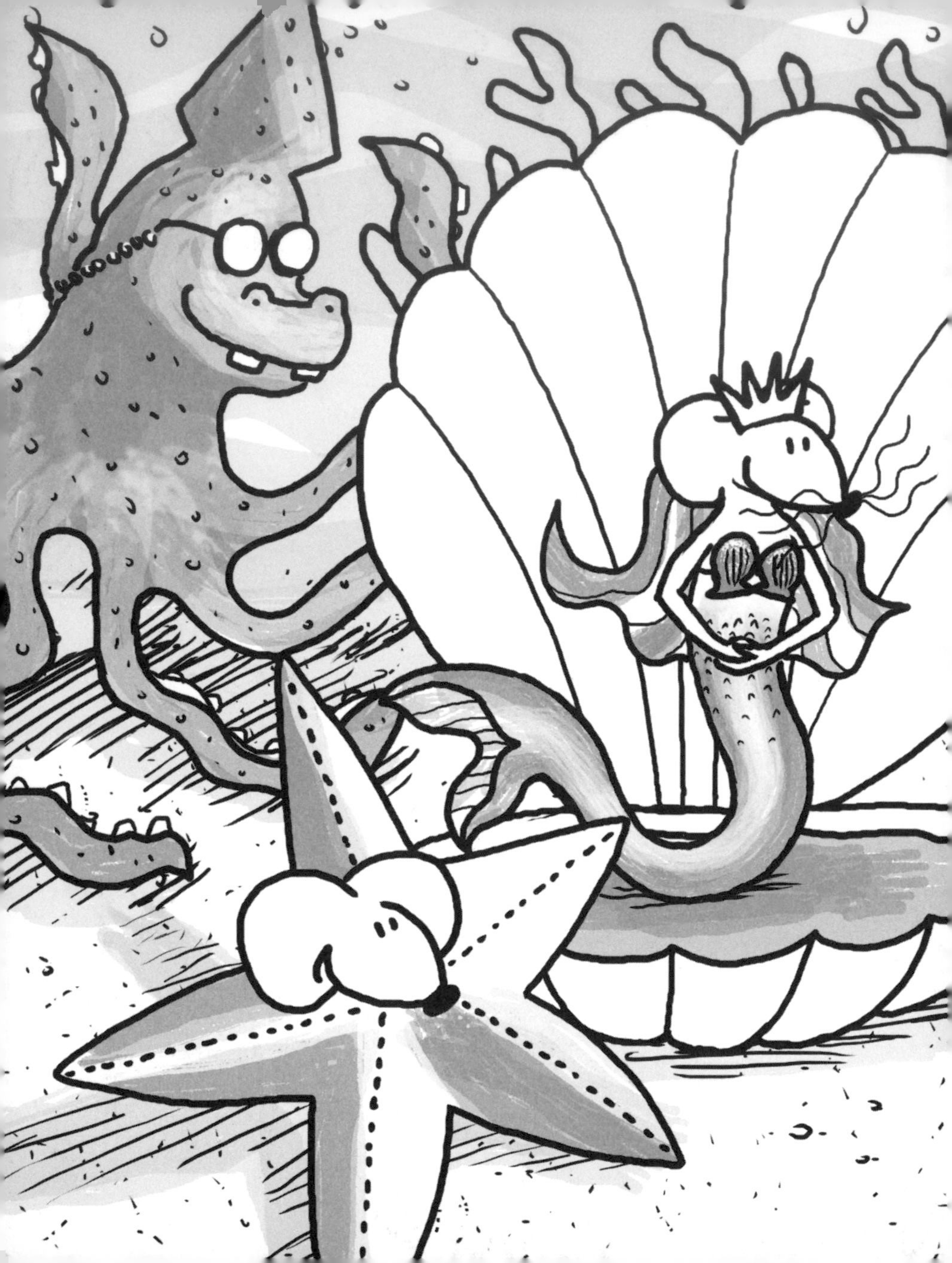

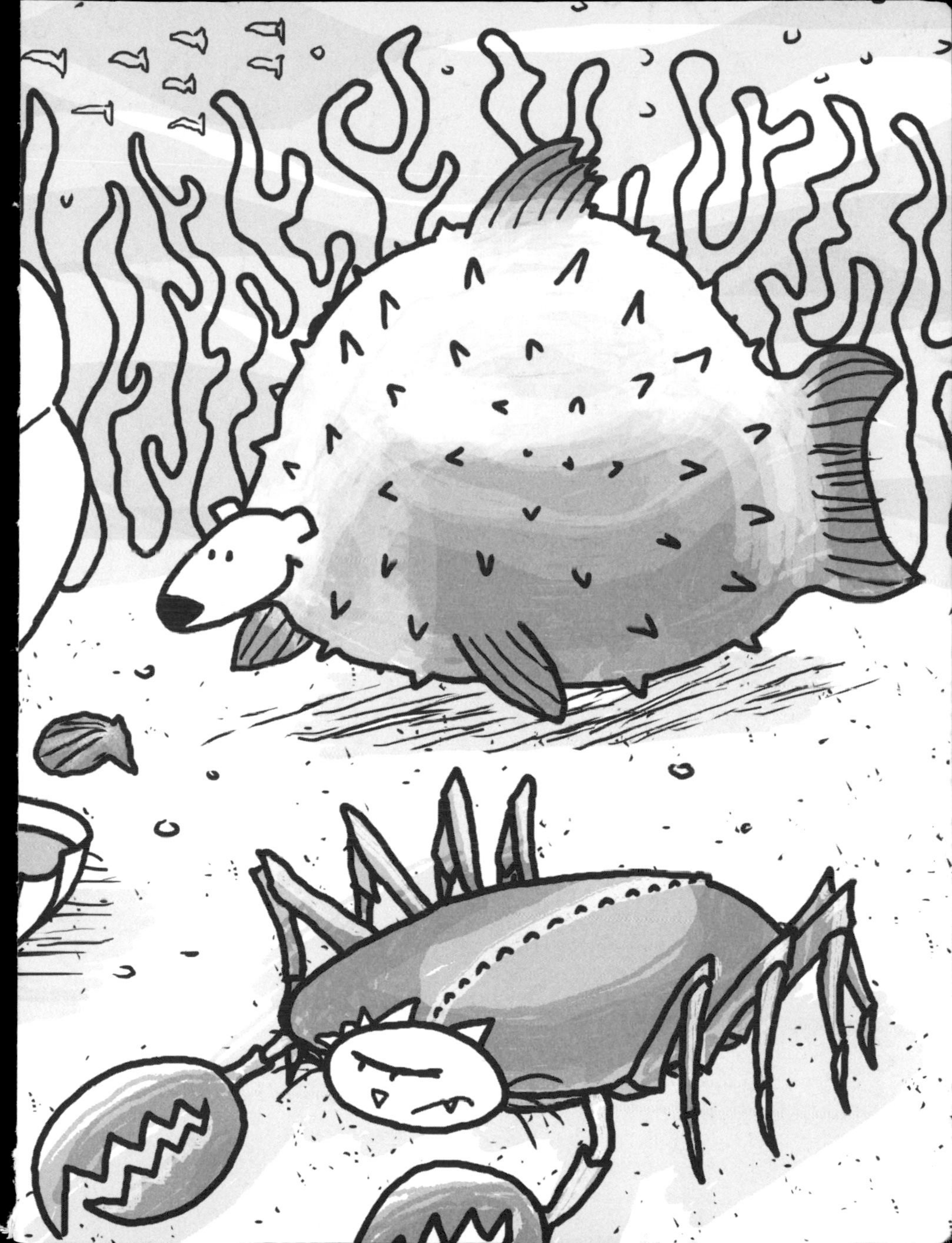

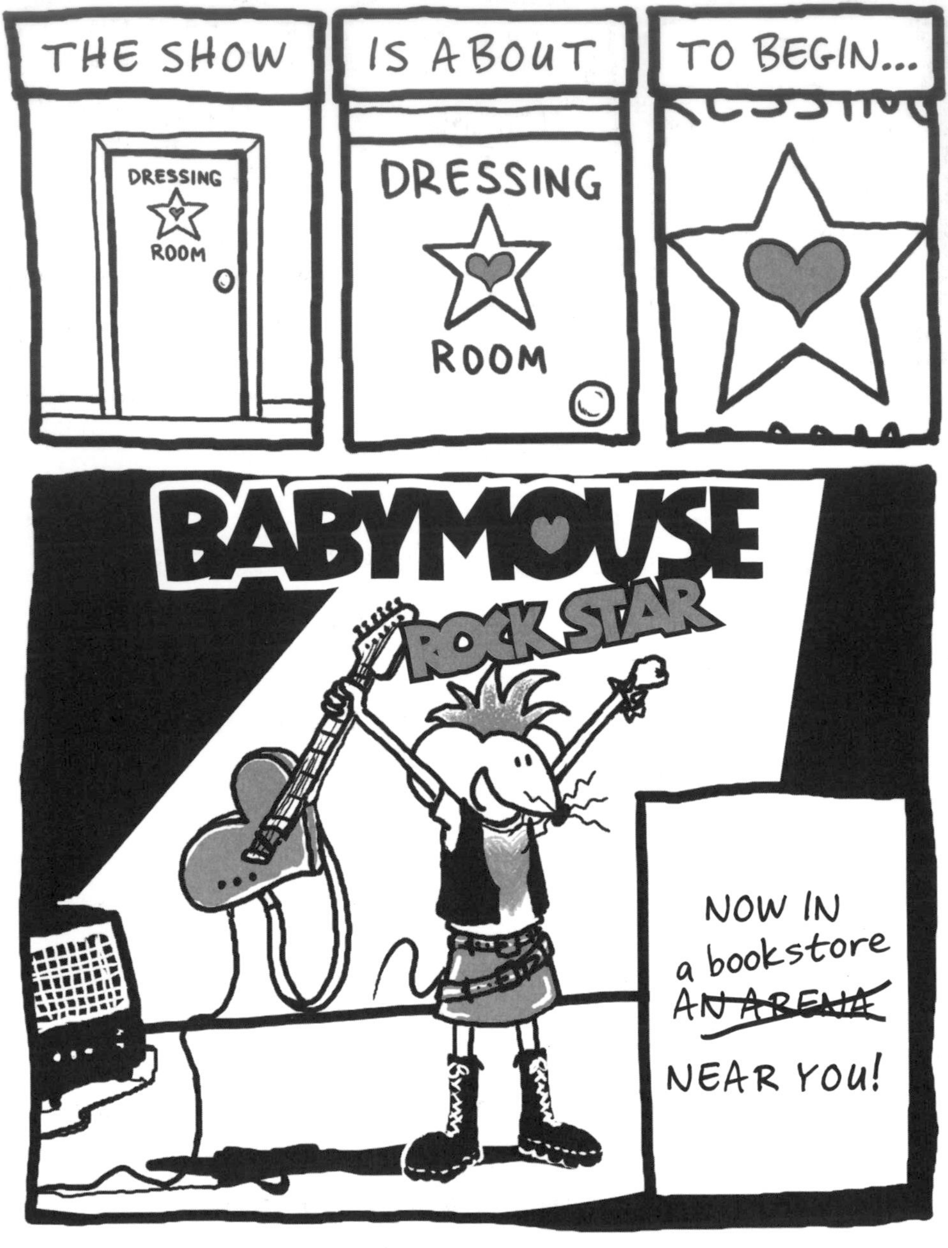
THE SHOW
IS ABOUT
TO BEGIN...
DRESSING
ROOM
DRESSING
ROOM
BABYMOUSE
ROCK STAR
NOW IN
a bookstore
~~AN ARENA~~
NEAR YOU!

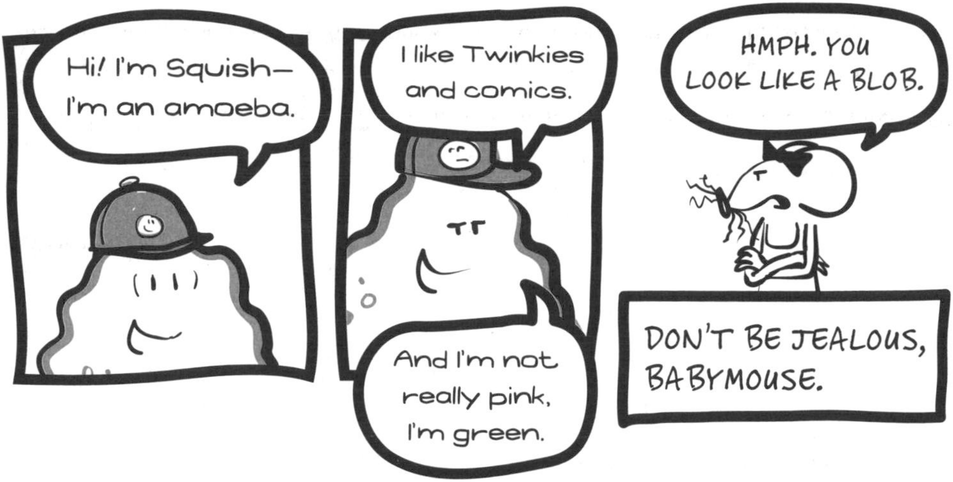
Hi! I'm Squish—
I'm an amoeba.
I like Twinkies
and comics.
And I'm not
really pink,
I'm green.
HMPH. YOU
LOOK LIKE A BLOB.
DON'T BE JEALOUS,
BABYMOUSE.

READ ABOUT SQUISH'S AMAZING ADVENTURES IN:

#1 SQUISH: Super Amoeba

#2 SQUISH: Brave New Pond

#3 SQUISH: The Power of the Parasite

#4 SQUISH: Captain Disaster

#5 SQUISH: Game On!

#6 SQUISH: Fear the Amoeba

#7 SQUISH: Deadly Disease of Doom

#8 SQUISH: Pod vs. Pod

★ "IF EVER A NEW SERIES DESERVED TO GO VIRAL, THIS ONE DOES."
—KIRKUS REVIEWS, STARRED

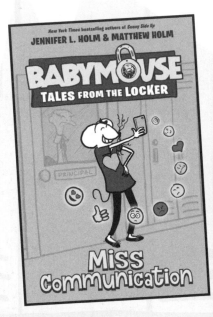